Cookie, The Pet Sitter

The Gobs of Pets Caper

Nancy Lewis Shelton

This is a work of fiction. Names, characters, and incidents are products of the author's imagination and are used fictitiously. Any resemblance to actual events, locales, or person, living or dead, is entirely coincidental.

No part of this book may be reproduced or stored in a retrieval system or transmitted in any form or by any means: electronic, mechanical photocopying, recording, or otherwise, without the express written consent of the author.

All cover animal graphics were adapted for use under the Creative Commons Share-Alike license. https://creativecommons.org/licenses/by-sa/3.0/

Cookie, The Pet Sitter ~ The Gobs of Pets Caper

Kindle Direct Publishing | Independently published

Copyright ©2021 Nancy Lewis Shelton

Cover and Interior Design by C.A. Simonson ©2021

ISBN: 9798755011457

ACKNOWLEDGEMENTS

When I was a child, I would complain about this or that. Mom would frown and say, "Nancy, things aren't always fair. You need to find the good in whatever life brings you." Now an aging adult, I still follow that advice.

During the 2020 pandemic, I spent many days cleaning closets and drawers. In my file cabinet, I found a book I began years ago. What if I edited and expanded on what I already had? Not only did I revise my earlier attempt, I learned much about how to improve my writing during the process. I have now begun book two of Cookie's pet sitting adventures.

Friends who proofed the rough drafts were excited about the story, and a couple of them suggested I should publish it. Then one of the Springfield Writers' Guild members read it and agreed. Cookie, the pet sitter, came to life for me.

Thanks to C. A. Simonson, who encouraged me and gave me tremendous assistance to bring my work to print. Additionally, I appreciate the time and efforts of all my friends who read one or more of the drafts. I hope you will enjoy *Cookie, The Pet Sitter* as much as they did.

Table of Contents

ACKNOWLEDGMENTS 3

CHAPTER ONE 7
    JUST CALL ME COOKIE

CHAPTER TWO 18
    LUNCH BUNCH

CHAPTER THREE 24
    DISASTER STRIKES

CHAPTER FOUR 35
    POLLY

CHAPTER FIVE 38
    LUNCH WITH OLIVIA

CHAPTER SIX 45
    OG THE DOG

CHAPTER SEVEN 50
    A RIDICULOUS CHIHUAHUA

CHAPTER EIGHT 58
    ADHD BULL TERRIER

CHAPTER NINE 66
    VISITING WINNIE

CHAPTER TEN 71
    NOSY NORA

CHAPTER ELEVEN 82
    POLLY'S GIRLS

CHAPTER TWELVE	88
GOBS OF PETS	
CHAPTER THIRTEEN	99
THE INTRUDER	
CHAPTER FOURTEEN	111
TOO MUCH DUCT TAPE	
CHAPTER FIFTEEN	118
THE LIE	
CHAPTER SIXTEEN	124
HOME AT LAST	
CHAPTER SEVENTEEN	131
SQUARE DANCE FUN	
CHAPTER EIGHTEEN	138
HELP FOR COOKIE	
CHAPTER NINETEEN	150
DOWN THE TRASH CHUTE	
CHAPTER TWENTY	162
THE RESCUE	
ABOUT THE AUTHOR	173

CHAPTER ONE
JUST CALL ME COOKIE

One Tuesday afternoon, my first, and possibly only, pet sitting job began. Juanita Lopez, the owner, had introduced me to Henry, her black Labrador, the week before. I used a security code to enter the gated community and another for the garage. There I opened the connecting door to the house. The Lab charged toward me, wiggled his hind end, and raced away for a toy. He dropped a squeaky clown for me to throw, shaking the thing so hard I expected pieces to fly around the room.

"My goodness! You are excited. Let's go to the backyard."

We played ball for a few minutes, then Henry roamed the yard while I read the owner's notes about caring for the dog, plants, and home. I smiled, noticing the loaf of banana bread beside her payment for me. Bubbling with excitement, I squealed at the amount on the substantial check, reflecting on what to buy with the extra money. Perhaps, best to save it for a laptop to replace my ancient computer.

Instead, I might start a travel fund. Since retirement from teaching kindergarten, selling my house, and moving to an apartment, I had considered the possibility of a second career. What an incredible opportunity to try pet sitting. Juanita owned a fun Lab and lived in a spacious home. There would be a week of plush living in the state-of-the-art kitchen, two living areas, and four bedrooms, each with its own bath, plus a pass to the community clubhouse and swimming pool. Although I treasured my new apartment, this stay resembled a week's vacation.

When Henry barked, I opened the door, jerking aside when the Lab bounded into the house. He dashed from one room to the other in frenzied zoomies, then outside again. I recalled how my own dog, now deceased, had once knocked me down as she zoomed. After eight laps in the yard, Henry ran to the kitchen for a drink from his water dish. Then we had snacks. His were two of those curly things with a bacon scent. He munched them down and jumped on me in an effort to steal my potato chips. That dog had no manners!

Henry calmed after the chips were gone. He followed me as I wandered through all the rooms to admire the posh furniture, knick-knacks, and artworks. In the basement living area, I crowded around a pool table to reach the leather-bound books shelved in a magnificent walnut bookcase. I hunted the possibilities for bedtime reading selecting *Go Set A Watchman*. Our last stop was in the guest bedroom, where the dog and I would have king-sized comfort for five nights.

The next morning, Henry prowled in the yard while I prepared his gourmet dog chow and laid a fat chew bone beside his dish. He trotted inside to gulp his breakfast, and I proceeded to the second-floor with a cup of coffee. There a small deck overlooked the half-acre yard. I reclined in an outdoor lounge chair while a breeze cooled my cheeks. Below, ostentatious dog statures guarded dozens of flower beds with emerging spring growth. Awesome!

Henry whined to join me, pressing his nose against the glass on the other side of the door. Juanita had mentioned he liked to watch the birds and squirrels. The Lab waited while I jiggled the door's knob to the left, then to the right, again to the left. I pulled, pushed, and kicked with no luck. Couldn't blame Juanita — not her fault I didn't check for an automatic lock. There was no visible way to climb up or, in my case, down. Although houses lay on each side of the property with more across the street, the well-groomed yards were void of people.

If I jumped from the second floor, I'd break a body part or cause brain damage.

Henry fussed again, his piercing brown eyes questioning me. "Sorry, it's locked," I said to the dog. "Go chomp on your treat."

What a disaster! In my head, I heard Mom's voice. *Focus on the positive.* I'll try, Mom. When I made another attempt to escape, I had no success. Phooey! All modern-day seniors had cell phones, except me. Whenever my only daughter, Marsha, called from Fairbanks, she reminded me for the umpteenth time to buy one. But my landline worked fine. Why mess with contract hassles? One reason was obvious – to escape this darn deck. There I stood, Cassandra Garrison, barefoot, dressed in Snoopy pajamas. I finger-combed my hair, pulled up the loose bottoms, and surveyed the surroundings, hoping for another person. Soon, on the sidewalk parallel to the street, a blond-haired fellow rode a bicycle within shouting distance.

"Please help!" I screamed.

The young man shook his head and pedaled away. It seemed an eternity before another opportunity approached – an older woman leading a gorgeous Golden Retriever.

I waved and yelled, "I'm locked out. Do you have a phone?"

She looked up at me. "Are you serious? Doesn't everyone?"

I blew out air and tried again. "Do you have a cell phone with you?"

"Of course, don't you?" She held hers up for me to see.

"Please call my friend. Tell her Cookie needs help. The number is...."

The walker ignored me to punch on her cell, probably for more important calls. Guess no choice but to wait for the next potential rescuer.

Almost immediately, a fire truck zoomed down the street in my direction. More sirens blared in the distance, becoming louder each minute. Darn. The realization hit me. The female walker had dialed 9-1-1! The heat on my cheeks intensified as I tugged my pajama bottoms again. Within fifteen minutes, emergency vehicles were parked by the fence as policemen, firemen, and medics packed the yard. My deceased mother taunted me again. *It could be worse.* Hmm. I guess someone could climb the drainpipe to mug me, but they wouldn't get much.

Passers-by and neighbors gathered to chat and point at the old woman in her pajamas. I threw my hands over my eyes as chills flooded my body. Slow breathing lessened my embarrassment, but only slightly. When I peeked through my fingers, I counted over twenty first responders and observers gathered below. A fireman positioned a tall ladder and then motioned for me to climb down. No way! If I made that precarious descent, I couldn't hold up my pajamas. That would be worse than jumping onto one of those air mattress things. Why hadn't I dressed? Why no cell phone? Why this job? *Are you ready for the newspaper film crew?* Mom, that's not encouragement.

Then the memory of the notes on the counter alerted me to another possibility. I yelled at the mob below and pointed to the house on the east side. "The neighbor has a key. See if they're home."

Fifteen minutes later, two policemen opened the deck's door. The older one had an engraved name tag that said Bob Hope and the younger, Tom Jones. My deceased husband, a fan of both the comedian and the singer, must have played a practical joke on me.

Officer Tom stared when I burst into uncontrolled laughter. "Don't say it," he said.

"Say what? Do you know each other?" asked his partner.

Officer Tom gave me a puzzled look. "Don't you have a cell phone with you?"

The Gobs of Pets Caper

Must be the only person in Springfield, Missouri, without one. "No. I'm the pet sitter. Didn't plan to be locked out here, and I don't own a cell."

Officer Hope frowned. "Do you own a coffee pot? The one at the station blew up. I need coffee. I need coffee now!"

"What? There's a fresh pot in the kitchen downstairs."

"We'll meet you there. Change your clothes. I'll pour the coffee. You'll need your driver's license to prove you're not a felon."

Henry pranced, trying to convince someone to notice him but had no luck. He dropped his bone and followed the men. My license? Why? I determined it was best not to question the police. Officer Bob didn't seem too agreeable, although the prospect of coffee could change that.

I hustled to dress and found my license. When I entered the kitchen, Officer Hope was adjacent to the coffee pot, slicing banana bread. His gray hair and protruding middle suggested he might be near retirement. Maybe his years of police work allowed him to make himself at home, or maybe he was just a grumpy old man who lived on coffee and sweets.

Officer Jones appeared to be a lost teenager rather than a policeman, but as I aged, the younger generation all looked like children. Sighing, he raised his eyebrows and both arms, a comment on his partner's intrusion. He set three mugs of coffee and a plate of sliced banana bread onto the table. Henry wagged his tail and waited, intending to seize any food that hit the floor.

The policemen examined my license, then told Tom, "Check Cassandra Garrison's record." In a low, gruff tone he added, "Cassandra, explain why no one in the yard knows you."

I shrugged. "Officer, most people call me Cookie."

"Quit avoiding the question." He slammed his fist on the table. "The neighbors down there said the owner, Juanita Lopez, has vanished. Where is she?"

What a kook! I jerked and spit out an answer. "I'm the pet sitter, taking care of the dog. She took a vacation."

Officer Jones burst through the door. "Let's go. She's clean. We have a real emergency, a northside shooting." The elder officer drained his mug and picked up another piece of banana bread, probably sorry dumb Cookie Garrison wasn't his crook of the day.

"I really appreciate your assistance," I said.

The younger guy stopped to reply. "That's what we're here for. Thanks for the snack. Sorry about his...."

"Shut up. Come on!" interrupted his partner.

Five minutes later, they were in their cruiser off to more exciting crimes but satisfied with my record check and the banana bread. I exhaled and sighed. Time to give back the key.

"Henry, out!" I tossed a tennis ball across the lawn, and the dog pursued it. Just as the gate opened, the neighbor's garage door rolled up, and a woman backed a Lexus onto the driveway. Embarrassed, my ears turned beet-red when I gave the driver the house key. She frowned but said nothing about my stupidity.

There were no more disasters that week, but soon I realized Juanita hadn't trained her two-year-old Lab. Sometimes, Henry sat on command but not always. He didn't understand that shoes weren't for chewing and dug craters in the yard. At night, he reclined on the foot of the bed but awakened at dawn to play ball. By mid-morning, he'd had a nap – not an ambitious schedule for a young dog. Labs were often voted the most loyal and smartest breed of dogs. How much could he learn in less than a week?

The next morning Henry attempted to climb onto my breakfast plate, then raced around the kitchen with one of my shoes. "Henry! Drop it! Bring!" He ignored me until I began to break Milk Bone biscuits into pieces. He dropped the shoe and sat in front of me.

Ahh, the secret to Henry's behavior was food. He'd benefit from manners lessons which I started immediately. The Lab was an enthused learner, responding quickly to my training. Before time for me to leave, he obeyed sit, come, down, stay, and no without any hesitancy. He even responded to hand signals. However, all that required lots of time and treats.

I enjoyed the king-sized bed, televisions in all the rooms, and training Henry as well as a tour of the neighborhood. But, every day, I left to go to my two-bedroom apartment. There I refreshed the food dish, changed the water, and scooped the litter box for my cat, Sparky. He'd been with me for five years, ever since he was abandoned on my front porch. When no one claimed him, I kept him. He had chosen me to be his human. Each time I left, he yowled, causing me a brief flood of guilt.

By Sunday, I was eager to be home. Henry's owner might recommend me for future pet sitting, but after the neighbors updated her on my escapades, probably not. Perhaps pet sitting wasn't the best choice for me. However, just in case, I picked up a notebook to organize Juanita's contact information. At the bottom of the page, I added: pack a bathing suit and review Henry's commands.

At that time, I didn't anticipate the predicaments looming ahead if pet sitting became my new career choice.

CHAPTER TWO

LUNCH BUNCH

Sunday night, I tucked into bed at ten o'clock. As usual, Sparky woke me at six Monday morning. If I insisted, he'd go to sleep, but no reason for me to stay in bed. "Even when you're a pest, I love you. It's lunch bunch day. That's as exciting as killing flies."

I stumbled into the kitchen and inhaled the aroma of coffee brewing in the automatic maker. When my husband, Carl, was alive, he cooked breakfast most mornings, eager to emphasize it was the most important meal of the day. What I fixed now was quick and easy. That morning, it was a toasted raisin bagel slathered with cream cheese. *You know that's not a nutritious breakfast.*

"Could be worse, Mom. It's veggies for lunch and dinner. Outside, Sparky."

He tore across the living room toward the sliding glass door that led to the deck. Some people say cats don't understand human talk, but most just tend to ignore their owners. They can be as unpredictable as lightning strikes.

Mother Nature announced the best season of the year, spring. After a dreary, frigid winter, crocus plants had begun to push through the damp ground. Budding trees along the walking path pronounced leaves were on the way. The cool spring air refreshed my attitude and removed the gloom I'd felt from adjusting to many losses.

Beyond the parking lot, birds chirped, and the caw of a crow echoed in the distance. The cat's body stiffened, and his ears perked up. A flock of honking Canada geese flew downward toward a pond, coming within inches of the apartment. The cat jumped off his perch, rested his paws on the railing, and stretched upward as the plane of birds prepared to land. I laughed at his antics. "Aren't they majestic? Sometimes I miss our house, but this is a terrific location, and that walking trail is impressive." I planned to take a stroll on it, but then, didn't know how stressful my first walk would be.

Oops! Didn't want to be late for lunch bunch, a gathering of several retired teacher friends. In the bedroom, I caught a magenta top as it tipped from its hanger. The silky material reminded me of Carl's smile when he gave it to me, a present on my birthday six years ago – the week before a drunk driver smashed into his car. No reason to preserve it. The blouse with my aqua pants created an attractive outfit.

Many of my husband's and mother's belongings had rested in a Goodwill receptacle for a while, but this top and a few other mementos kept both Carl and Mom in my thoughts. In my head, I often heard Mom but not my husband. However, when I first woke in the morning, Carl sometimes seemed to be in the bed beside me. It felt real, but I knew it wasn't.

In the bathroom, I observed my five-foot, four-inch frame in the mirror, resisting the reflection's message that I needed to lose at least twenty pounds. The older I got, the harder it was to drop the weight. However, at sixty-five, my appearance surpassed many of my aging acquaintances. *It's not healthy to starve yourself.* Mom, there's no plan to do that.

Sparky jumped onto the counter, impatient for the water to splash into the sink. From a tray, I removed shimmering red lipstick and liquid Cover Girl – no mascara. Although it darkened the blue of my eyes, it made them sting. Noticing more gray hairs peeking through the dark brown ones, I flipped on the curling iron. Must call for a color and cut appointment. My ears were no longer pierced, but a pair of gold clip earrings finished my outfit.

On my way down the stairs to the first floor, I hesitated. I'd forgotten the photos for the lunch bunch gals. Darn, better go back. I'm not old enough for these senior moments. The envelope with pictures sat on the end of the kitchen bar. I got it and hurried down the hall toward the stairs – more exercise and quicker than waiting on the elevator.

Thirty minutes later, I arrived at the Happy Fisherman and, after an additional five, found a parking spot. In the restaurant entrance, I admired several paintings and enormous tanks of tropical life. A strong scent permeated the air – a light fishy smell mixed with a more pleasant one, perhaps vanilla. This restaurant wasn't my choice for the lunch bunch gals, but it wasn't my turn to choose a place.

Nora Alexander waved at me from a corner table. She yelled, "You're late. We can't order till you're here."

I wanted to say "shut up" but managed to quell that desire. *Be nice. You can't take back words or stuff toothpaste back into the tube.* Mom, did anyone ever do that?

Not willing to admit the tardiness was my fault, I replied, "Uh, sorry, problem with the cat." My face flushed at the fib because eliminating all little white lies was one of my new year's resolutions. Needed to work on that one.

Lunch with this group had been a first and third Monday event since my retirement. Though sometimes bored, I went because my two best friends were always there. Over the top of my menu, I studied one, Polly Andrews. Shorter and plumper than the other gals, she had a pleasing face with dewy green eyes that sparkled through silver-framed glasses. In contrast, she wore an out-of-style matching suit. Though faded and old, it wasn't bedraggled. Perhaps at our age, comfort was more important than style.

As kindergarten teachers, we had shared laughter, frustrations, and teaching ideas when we worked in the same building. Then she announced her retirement. I took the plunge too, but she had a husband, pets, and family in Missouri. Still did, but me – no longer a husband, no close family, and only one cat. All of my family lived in Alaska or California.

Next to Polly sat loud-mouthed Nora. Why was she part of this group? Not a retired teacher, she worked part-time in a government office. Her brownish eyes looked buggy under oversized glasses. Her hair never changed – faded, brown and poufy on the top. If a wig, she'd better buy a new one. *Be positive. Seek the best in your friends.* Thanks, Mom. That's number two of my resolutions.

During the last luncheon, tired of the meaningless banter, I had invented nicknames for the gals — Pet Lover Polly, Nosy Nora, and Outstanding Olivia, my other best friend. Pearl button earrings accented her meticulous makeup. The top of her class in high school, college, and graduate school, she had mentored me through classes and a long career of teaching. Both Polly and Olivia supported me when I had more than my share of blows.

Beside Olivia, Marge Smith glittered in a raucous purple, low-cut top that emphasized her ample breasts. I'd be uncomfortable in her tight, provocative attire, but not Manhunter Marge. Silver-hooped earrings vibrated, making a bell sound when she laughed. She claimed that she taught Spanish for over twenty years, but I wondered. Nora had spread rumors about Marge's many affairs, but those were none of my concern. Several other lunch bunchers seldom ate with us. Not sure why I wanted to be there either — hated fish, missed relaxing on my deck, and allowed Nora to irritate me.

As it turned out, great food and a bit of hilarity filled the rest of my afternoon at the Happy Fisherman.

CHAPTER THREE

DISASTER STRIKES

When Amile arrived for our lunch orders, Marge motioned to him. "A question for a handsome waiter. She pushed her flaming red hair behind her ears and hid beneath the menu to whisper to the server. When she patted his arm, he suppressed a laugh.

"Hey, we're hungry," said Olivia. "Flirt later." Amile wrote Marge's order on a pad before he proceeded to the rest of us. I selected the only non-seafood item on the menu, a green salad with grilled chicken.

"Cookie, is that a new top?" asked Marge. "I adore that color on you."

"No, but I don't wear it often."

"Why not? It makes you look hot."

I didn't reply. Realizing the earrings caused my ears to throb, I threw them into my purse, wondering why I had on earrings or the "hot" blouse.

Nora reached across the table to slam her hand in front of me. "You must eat fish twice a week. I believe..."

Good friend Polly interrupted the woman's blather to veer us to another topic. "Cookie, tell us a kindergarten story."

"Let's see. Once our principal encouraged us to involve the kids when we made our classroom rules. Little Julie said, 'Listen to the adults.' Other children contributed ideas, then Alan added, 'Don't swing from the bathroom pipes.' At recess, I sent the janitor to the basement. There, several boys hung on the ceiling pipes in the bathroom. After that, we stuck to my rules."

"How's your family, Cookie?" asked Marge.

"Marsha and Chet still teach in Fairbanks. They're contented there, but I miss seeing my grandkids."

"Why don't you visit them? Alaska would be a superb trip."

"March is not the best month to vacation that far north. Besides, it's time for me to find a part-time job."

"Why? Dance. Travel. Play more bridge. Meet a new guy. Have fun."

Nosy Nora added, "You have your retirement income and Carl's insurance. Other people need work more than you. Anyway, what can you do?"

Unfortunately, there was no insurance, but savings and profits from my sold mortgage-free house provided an adequate income, and Missouri retirement payments were great. Money wasn't the issue. Except for volunteering at the nursing home, my life had become stagnant, one without enough purpose.

Olivia gave Nora a perfect teacher stare, a vicious scowl with wrinkled eyebrows. She said in her firmest manner, "Stop criticizing Cookie. You need to shut up."

Nora slumped and lowered her head, "Sorry, just trying to help."

All of us, except Nora, had a stern expression and supporting body language. Perhaps that came naturally for teachers. During my first assignment, a school-supplied paddle on my desk gave the same result, but I hated that threat. Behavior management and teaching lessons required both experience and instinct. With support from my two friends, I developed skills that worked most of the time without relying on physical punishment.

Amile delivered our food, setting in front of me an enormous bowl with a variety of greens, almonds, cranberries, apples, pineapple, and mounds of chicken. Wow. Then, he picked up Polly's and Nora's orders from a cart. As Nora shoved her chair backward, she didn't see Amile behind her. She stood up at the same time he leaned over to put down the plates.

Wham! Amile rammed into Nora. Her chair clattered sideways onto the floor. She held onto the table to keep from falling, but the impact of the collision caused her wig to fly off her head and land on Polly's Salmon Surprise. For a few seconds, the room was quieter than a morgue, but I failed to stifle my giggles. The uproar around me intensified as the rest of the gals, as well as customers at other tables, hooted with laughter.

Nora's skin was the shade of a bleached bedsheet. She sobbed and ran toward the restroom, bumping into chairs and people in her dash to escape the calamity.

Marge said, "Hey, Amile. We have a dead rodent on the Salmon Surprise. Bring another order, please."

The waiter froze beside the overturned chair; all color drained from his face. "I'm, I'm so sorry. I, will she be okay?"

"Sure. We all have a catastrophe once in a while. Amile, look at me. Pick up the chair, and get Polly a fresh plate of food."

I smiled. She had been a teacher.

Olivia lifted the deceased hair piece from its new home and along with Nora's purse, left. "I'd better comfort her."

"Tell her we're sorry about the laughter," I said.

Marge snickered, "I'm not. She had it coming. Did you cause that, Polly?"

Polly shook her head. "Of course not. You need to be more empathic. How would you feel if...?"

"Never mind. Get over it. As the psychic of this group, you predict the mishaps of the rest of us. Guess you didn't see that one coming. Where's my camera?" She dug in her bag until she found a large zoom monstrosity.

Pieces of hair and bobby pins poked above the baked potato and salmon patty, some at attention, tiny soldiers preparing for an attack. Marge snapped several photographs of the mess before Amile brought two fresh plates.

"Why are you taking pictures?" asked Polly.

"I'm documenting the day. Why?" answered Marge.

"Please don't post them on social media."

"Nuts! Too bad the wig is gone. That was spectacular!"

We watched as Olivia ushered Nora out the front door. Marge joked, but no one laughed. Even though I often hated Nora's actions, my stomach lurched in pain for her.

Olivia returned to her seat and ate a bite of tilapia. "Eat up. Nora's leaving, but she'll be here the next time.

Marge, you'd better not put those photos on Instagram or anywhere else. Got it?"

Marge zipped her fingers across her mouth, but we all knew she seldom followed our recommendations. A stunned silence settled around the table with Nora's fresh plate of food untouched, reminiscent of her anguish. My salad was delicious, but I didn't relax until the staff cleared the table. When a different waiter came for our dessert orders, I speculated about the extra calories. In my mind, I saw Mom's disapproval. However, when the other gals ordered, I didn't resist the Chocolate Delight.

"Where's Amile?" Marge asked the replacement waiter.

"Uh, he's on break."

"Tell him he did nothing wrong. Be sure he gets our tips."

Soon, the new server brought each of us a shiny square dessert plate. Mine had an enormous brownie topped with vanilla ice cream, dark syrup, and a spurt of whipped cream. They all melted together to create a smooth chocolate taste. Yum!

As we enjoyed our desserts, chatting began again, mostly about illness, grandchildren, and the failures of today's youth. What would we be doing at eighty-plus years? Now, we jumped from one topic to another, often not listening to each other. It boggled my mind.

I rose. "Sorry about Nora, but what an impressive lunch. Thanks, Olivia."

Marge's high heels clicked on the wooden floor until she reached me. She leaned close and whispered, "See you at bridge or sooner to go dancing."

Why did Marge say that again? Bridge, yes! Dancing, no!

Polly asked, "Are you sure Sparky is all right?"

"He's wonderful. Come over. You and I are his favorite people."

"I'll do that. Call you soon."

On the way home, I pondered what to do with my spare time. Did I want a job or more volunteering? I'd regret becoming too busy for bridge games and an occasional lunch bunch meal. Should I plan a vacation – maybe a trip to California. My sister, Tammy, might invite me there or have thoughts about jobs for me. At home, I composed an e-mail to her.

> Hi, Sis. How's California? Maybe I can visit you soon. If that's not convenient, I'll look for a job. Suggestions on that? How about pet sitting?
>
> Cookie

The Gobs of Pets Caper

As I hit enter, the phone buzzed.

"Got your package," said my daughter Marsha. "Eli is fascinated with the motorized car." She chatted about teaching frustrations, then said, "Hang on for the kids."

Emma, age twelve, said, "Thank you for our diaries and colored pencils. We miss you. Can Elaine and I visit this summer?"

Yes! What fun to go to Silver Dollar City, the zoo, and a children's play at Little Theater! Might even consider an overnight to Six Flags in St. Louis. "Of course, any time."

After Eli and Elaine talked, Marsha added, "Emma's notion, but it might work. I'll send you possible dates, love ya."

Tears welled up as I searched for recent pictures of the children. Eli, age four, had his father's curly black poodle hair. Nine-year-old Elaine and older sister resembled Marsha, but their personalities were quite different. Elaine had inherited Marsha's gentleness, and Emma, her high intelligence. It had been several months since the family had come to Missouri. I missed them.

Tuesday morning, I checked my computer for new e-mails. The first was a reply from Tammy.

> Hi Sis, would be great to see you, but it's no fun here. The doctor proposed a new

```
procedure for my husband, Luke; pray he'll be
better in a few months. Try the Internet for
info on pet sitting. You'd enjoy that!
```

Hmm. No California vacation, but pet sitting might still be an option. I needed another opinion. Polly was an animal expert. Before marrying Albert, she had been a pet sitter. Also, her family had cared for many lost and abused animals – once even a wild duck hit by a car. Dogs, cats, fish, birds, rabbits, and various rodents resided in the huge five-bedroom Victorian house on an acre of ground. If someone abandoned a box of kittens or tied a lost dog to the porch railing, either new owners adopted them, or Polly kept the critters.

After the sixth ring, she answered, sounding breathless. "Working in the garden. So glad you called."

"I might become a pet sitter. Any advice?"

"Wait a while. It's not safe now."

"What do you mean not safe?"

"Pet sitting can be dangerous. Do you intend to stay by yourself in a strange place?"

Visions of being trapped on Juanita's deck flashed through my mind. "That won't bother me."

Silence followed a deep sigh.

"Are you there?" I asked.

"Yes. Okay, you're determined. Get information on the kinds and ages of all pets. You may have older animals that require shots or medications. People often have weird requests. Once I had to dispose of a dead possum. But, please consider waiting."

"What did you watch besides cats, dogs, and dead animals?"

She laughed. "Birds, a snake, iguanas. The birds were okay, but the snake ate live mice and the iguanas, giant cockroaches. But that was okay. Both owners gave me a generous bonus. Visit with the family. Meet their pets. All that before you say 'yes.'"

"Anything else?"

"Be sure to try out keys. Don't settle for a garage door opener. The electricity might shut off. Get liability insurance. Pets can be anxious, afraid of storms, eat odd things. Cats are tricky. They may have a favorite dish, refuse different food, and, weird though it seems, not eat if they can't see the bottom of the bowl. Many hate strangers, which can be a problem if you have to take them to a vet."

"Won't owners tell me potential concerns?"

"Not always. Also, make a quick trip to check the entire house before you leave – easy to miss an unwanted gift on a bed."

"Thanks. I haven't decided yet if pet sitting is for me."

"Cookie, this is not an auspicious period for you. Why not wait until fall?"

Ah-ha! I knew why she was apprehensive about my possible career choice. She had read my horoscope. I'd dealt with her warnings for many years but tended to ignore them.

At the computer, I consulted the Greene County Library website for books and requested *Pet Sitting for Beginners* and *Make Money Pet Sitting*. Other Internet sites stressed that the pet sitter needed liability insurance, business cards, and a website but I had no plans to buy all that.

If I'd known the future, I'd have trashed the library books and locked myself in the apartment with my cat.

CHAPTER FOUR

POLLY

A dream jolted Polly from a deep slumber. Her eyelids snapped open. She recalled a fuzzy picture of Albert, her two daughters, and four grandchildren with Cookie in the background. She had a vast knowledge of dream interpretation, but this one puzzled her. Did it have something to do with her family or with Cookie?

Since a child, premonitions, visions, and omens warned when events might happen to her or to those she knew. In third grade, she told a buddy to be careful on the playground. The girl ignored her and fell off the jungle gym, hitting her leg on a sharp rock. When the injury required stitches, the girl blamed Polly for the accident.

From then on, Polly was cautious about repeating her forewarnings to others. However, none of her family worried about the gift. They told tales about Aunt Alice, who had similar powers. Usually, they followed Polly's advice.

Although frustrated by not understanding the recent dream, she reassured herself these vague visions must be about Cookie. But, instead, could they be about a family member? No, it must be Cookie.

In the study, Polly removed horoscope references from a bookcase. In one of them, she located January 16, Cookie's birthday. She cried when she read the last paragraph: *This is a stressful period. You must be skeptical in all your pursuits. Be careful and avoid strangers. It is not an ideal month to begin new ventures, particularly if they involve travel. Be cautious in all you do.*

The warnings in the second book were worse, suggesting all new activities were extremely dangerous. Reading the horoscopes strengthened her anxiety about Cookie's safety but all she could do was to insist her friend wait a few months before starting a new venture.

After Polly cooked a breakfast of scrambled eggs with fried potatoes, she reached for the saltshaker. By accident, a pile of salt spilled onto the floor. While she cleaned up the mess, she tossed some over her left shoulder. That was the second bad omen in a week. Earlier, a picture, for no reason, fell off the wall. Plus,

Cookie had just moved; that meant danger if she pursued anything different too soon.

Polly knew that she was seldom wrong about her ability to predict trouble; however, she also was aware Cookie might not listen to any warnings.

CHAPTER FIVE
LUNCH WITH OLIVIA

On Tuesday night, loud animal cries jarred me awake. Darn cat. What did he want? My lean, coal-black feline halted at the bedroom door and yowled.

"Why are you up? It's midnight! You'll upset everyone in the building."

The food and water bowls were not empty. What could be wrong? His screeches, full of distress, intensified. I flicked on the light switch in the laundry room, ready to reprimand him, then noticed the cat pacing around his litter box. Uh-oh. The receptacle rested against the wall, lid on backward. After I adjusted the top, he jumped inside.

"Meow. Meow."

"Sorry. Guess I had another senior moment."

Might the desperate fellow potty someplace else? During the next fifteen minutes, I examined every corner of my apartment. All rooms were neat and tidy. In the guest bedroom, I admired Mom's furniture, glad I didn't sell it at my moving sale.

Back in my room, Sparky had curled onto a pillow. I slipped in bed beside him, but after thirty minutes, gave up on sleep and went to the living room to watch one of my favorite DVDs, *Men in Black*. Within minutes, the cat came to tuck his body behind my bent legs. Soon his tiny purr changed into a soft snore, lulling me to dreamland.

At 2:00 a.m. I bolted upright, aroused by a nightmare. For an elongated period, I was groggy, unaware of where I was. The stopped DVD player blinked. Apparently, the men in black succeeded in defending planet Earth without my assistance. My hands were clammy, and my face burned. In the bathroom, I pressed a wet washcloth against my forehead for a few minutes, then thought about the dream. Someone had tied up a female. Who? – one of my kindergarteners, a granddaughter, me? Was my subconscious attempting to tell me something? Polly would insist all dreams were warnings, but I didn't believe that.

Back in bed, I finally managed to sleep again, but at daylight, my feline friend chewed and pulled my hair. When I scolded him, he climbed onto my chest to push his feet in a rhythmic pattern. When I ignored that, he gave me a chin butt. A glint of bliss descended upon him as I kneaded the space between his ears, then stroked his neck. When the ringing phone interrupted our peaceful relaxation, I pushed Sparky aside to answer it.

"Let's have lunch at Sunrise Tea House today," said Olivia.

"Don't you have a book to finish?" Although I enjoyed hanging out with her, I didn't want to eat at a restaurant again that week.

"Yes, but we have to eat, and you need to talk."

"Who told you what?" I asked.

"Lunch today, yes, or no?"

"Yes, I'll meet you there at eleven."

At the Sunrise Tea Room, my mouth watered at the case of dessert choices displayed in the front. Behind me, Olivia said, "We'd better have a meal first."

"Have to skip dessert. I overdid it yesterday."

"Me too. Let's sit in the back so we can view the garden."

Even though it was early spring, annuals were in bloom. Through the window, we admired a border of square stones that surrounded assorted flowers. Red salvia bloomed around pansies, and marigolds hugged the salvia. In the center of the arrangement, a circle of assorted patterns of petunias added color. An unusual variety of trees completed the picturesque scene. The beauty awakened a delight I hadn't experienced in a while.

Olivia interrupted my thoughts. "What's bothering you?"

"Just because I left lunch bunch first? I just wanted to go home. The food was delicious, and Nora's flying wig, hilarious."

Olivia laughed. "Yep, but we need to be kinder to her. You were distant yesterday – uneasy, worried. What's wrong?"

"Don't know. My attitude needs an adjustment. Maybe just the winter blahs. Since I've moved, there's nothing I have to do. You're working on your second novel. Polly has gobs of projects. Marge, her newest beau. Don't know about the rest of the gals."

"You've been dealing with loss for a long time, a continual cycle of mourning and partial recovery. However, even when life has storms, the sunshine always follows."

"I know. After Carl's awful wreck and my square dance partner's cancer, I constantly thought about death. At times, I didn't want to go on living but had to plod on. Then Mom became ill, and my dog died. But now, I do try to reflect on all my blessings."

We both knew everything about each other, but for some reason, I needed to restate it all. My thoughts reverted to when I had to work, even when I couldn't eat or sleep. Then the darkness left, and my life lightened, but some days, it wasn't enough.

"You're daydreaming. Are you feeling sorry for yourself?"

"What? No, just pondering life's changes. You know life's ups and downs are similar to the game of bridge."

Olivia tipped her head and raised her eyebrows. "How's that?"

"There are great deals, so-so ones, and ghastly ones, but they are never the same. My life isn't bad, just a bit boring right now."

"You need to regroup. Bored — when your kindergarten kids said that word, what did you do?"

"Told them 'Boring is your choice.'"

Behind me, a giggle interrupted our discussion. A vivacious young server had heard my comment.

"Hi. My name's Martina. It's not boring here. We have an opening for another waitress. I'll bring you an application. Tips are incredible."

I giggled. "No way, I gave up that fun forty years ago. We both want broccoli-cheddar soup with a turkey sandwich."

The Gobs of Pets Caper

After the waitress hustled toward the kitchen, Olivia took a pad and a pen from an enormous black bag. "Let's brainstorm suggestions for your new life." She wrote square dance at the top of the paper.

"Not without a steady partner. Plus, I haven't been in ages."

"It's brainstorming. Don't analyze. Your turn."

I sighed, impatient with that exercise. "Get a job."

"Pet sitting?"

Then I knew she had talked to Polly.

Olivia scribbled pet sitting and volunteer onto her pad. "You could tutor in your old kindergarten room. Next?"

"How about a new boyfriend?"

Olivia frowned. "Skip that one. Next, entertaining?"

"Entertaining a boyfriend? No way!"

"No, Silly. Quit being difficult. You've had bridge parties, game nights, and once a mystery dinner."

"One more, and I'm done with this exercise. A trip to Alaska if the grandgirls aren't here this summer."

Olivia added travel and pushed the paper across the table. "Cheer up. A new passion is waiting for you."

I shoved the page into the bottom of my purse.

"Now do this," said Olivia. "Take a stance. Sit up straight, hold your head up, and smile. You'll gain confidence and your old zest for living."

After a fake smile, I yearned to change the subject. "Enough. What about you? Besides writing a book, what do you desire most?"

She raised her eyebrows, tucked in her bottom lip, and then smiled. "World peace, recognition as an author, and gobs of chocolate."

Martina was back. "We have chocolate here." She handed us dessert menus. "I saw you admire our goodies."

"My stance is no dessert," I said.

Olivia gave back the menus. "They look luscious, but not this time."

"All righty. Who claims the check?" asked Martina.

Olivia held out her hand. While she paid the bill, I dug in my purse for a tip. Next time, I'd pay.

Before we parted, Olivia reached for a hug. "Will you be at Marge's tomorrow?"

"Looking forward to it. Not giving up bridge."

I tend to overthink. Right or wrong, I didn't need assistance from Olivia or Polly. My life's choices were mine. But what if I made the wrong ones?

CHAPTER SIX

OG THE DOG

The next day, I dialed Polly's number. After the first ring, she answered.

"I decided to do more pet sitting," I said. "Thanks for your suggestions."

A deep moan traveled across the miles. "Why not wait a while? Vibes are negative about anything new. Let me read your horoscope."

"No. I'll catch you later."

"Don't hang up. Wait. Please call a gal who quit pet sitting."

"Sorry, not now. Got to go."

I hated being rude but didn't want to discuss her premonitions. Her daughters once warned me Polly knew the exact day a disaster would occur, but her fears won't rule my life. My plan for the day was to pick out designs for business cards and play an afternoon of bridge at Marge's. If it was not a decent game, I might consider Polly's bad omens.

What a lucky bridge day! My cards were unbelievable with three slams, each with a different partner, plus many bid games. After the fifth round, my phenomenal total beat all the other players. By the end of seven games, my scorecard showed 8,100 points, a record for this group. Marge presented me with the first prize, a colorful wreath with yellow, red, and white flowers. What a lucky day! Perhaps I'd buy some lottery tickets.

At four o'clock, I balanced library books, purse, and wreath while I searched for my apartment key. Inside, yowls expressed the cat's anticipation or perhaps irritation. Even when obnoxious, pets bring out the best qualities in humans. Soon he'd be on my lap purring to show he loved me.

The next day, I stopped at the print shop for my cards. When I examined them, a warm, pleasant feeling flowed into my body. My name was placed in swirled letters among pictures of kittens and puppies on a bright yellow background. Soon, all seventy of the apartment doors held one of the gorgeous cards. Many pets inhabited my building, but only a small number of owners would hire me.

On Friday, I had my first response from an elderly lady, Eunice Taylor, in apartment 110. She had twisted her ankle and needed a dog walker for a few days. The week before, I'd met her outside with a mixed-breed dog, Og. If I did a stupendous job, she might be my first positive reference.

As I neared her apartment, I noticed Eunice at the open door, propped behind a walker. She was about five feet tall and weighed less than a hundred pounds. Her face resembled a big raisin, with wrinkles twisting in strange patterns. She wore a long dress with a bib-style apron. It reminded me of my grandmother's outfits.

Eunice Taylor motioned to me. "Come in, dear. Hate this walker, but I can still make us tea while you get better acquainted with my darling Og." She pointed to a rocking chair. "Have a seat."

I needed to get over the uneasy feeling I had when meeting a new client, but the fragrance of bread baking and her graciousness calmed my nerves. Og ran over to greet me with one bark and a joyful, doggy smile. He had a blue eye and one brown one with skin showing through his minimal hair. That, combined with a lengthy tail, produced a hilarious-looking fellow. He'd win most ugly dog contests. But one shouldn't judge people or dogs by how they look. A charmer, I fell in love with him as he retrieved a tennis ball to drop at my feet. He needed no commands to pick it up, bring it back, and wait for me to praise him.

When Mrs. Taylor said, "Sit," he plopped onto the floor to wait until the lead snapped shut on his collar. He didn't pull, seldom barked more than once, and parked his back for a scratching when we finished our outings. Og was a wonderful dog, maybe because his owner was a wonderful person. After five days of fun with the dog and occasional tea times, Eunice Taylor presented me with a generous check. "There's a little bonus, dear. You did an excellent job. I want you to call me Eunice; I think we can be friends."

Nodding, I thanked her and sped away to my apartment. When I opened the door, I waved the check at Sparky. He attacked it.

I snatched it away before he could reach it. "Hey, what's that about?"

Later, no longer upset, my feline curled into a ball on my lap. As I scratched his head, my thoughts veered to Polly's warnings. It had been a while since her premonitions included me. Then I recalled that several years before when, in a dream, she saw me fall. My friend warned me not to roller skate at a school party. I ignored her warnings, fell, and broke my arm, but I had never considered it possible that she knew my skate would hit a chunk of gum and cause me to ram into the wall.

After that memory, a dark and foreboding sense of danger made me tremble. Could she be correct this time?

CHAPTER SEVEN

A RIDICULOUS CHIHUAHUA

My answering machine blinked to signal a new message. "This is Nick Anderson. Our regular dog sitter canceled. Please call. We need someone beginning tonight."

Sparky yowled and pawed at my leg when Nick repeated his number.

"Cat, I'm losing patience with you!"

His tail jerked, and his green eyes gazed into mine. He had a smug look, as if he might not approve of my pet sitting. I gathered him into my arms until he calmed.

"Here's a joke? How do you spell mousetrap with three letters?"

He stared at me as if he didn't know the answer.

"C. A. T. It'll be fine, boy. You'll always be my number one pet." He reached his paws onto my chest for a cat hug, adding a loud purr that reminded me of a swarm of mosquitoes. I phoned Nick Anderson and agreed to meet him at his father's house as soon as I could get there.

After the first stoplight, I marveled at the Walmart parking lot, packed with cars, where not long before, there had been a field of hay. Bet I could get a job there, but why would I? Farther, groves of trees dressed in new leaves framed the road. The Missouri Ozarks would soon become a land of multiple colors and aromas. I loved spring when nature awakened to give rebirth, when tulips bloomed, and the aroma of honeysuckle tickled my nose.

When the driver of an oncoming car honked, I swerved the Buick into the correct lane. *If you don't concentrate, you'll soon join me.* Mom had a strange sense of humor. I curved onto Blossom Street and watched for the address as I passed rows of brick one-story homes. Exquisite lawns and flower beds brightened many yards, but at the Anderson's house, only a few colorful daffodils rose above the rotten vegetation.

A tall, distinguished-looking man in a dark suit waited in the front yard. When I approached him, strong fumes of aftershave wafted toward me. They reminded me of Carl.

"Hi, I'm Nick," he said. "Come in to meet my father, George, and his dog, Fluffy."

As I entered the Anderson's house, the uneasy feeling came back. What were all these people doing? Was that a friendly Chihuahua on the old man's lap? I hadn't asked the dog's breed or anything else. The father, a bald man who must be at least ninety, reclined in a blazing red lift chair. He stared at me through thick glasses but didn't smile or speak. Fluffy was an unusual name for his dog, but it was a perfect description of the inside of the living room. Shelves and tables overflowed with knick-knacks, baskets, and lamps with lace on the shades. For some reason, all the stuff added to my discomfort as I recalled what Polly had said about not staying in strange homes.

Nick motioned to a line of chairs. "Take a seat. Coffee or tea?"

"Neither, thank you."

He sat across from me on the edge of a sofa. "Sorry for such short notice. Our regular sitter was hospitalized with pneumonia. We hope you can bring Fluffy inside before dark beginning today, then out each morning. Dad has an appointment at the Med Center in St. Louis. I'll call with more about our plans. Okay to pay you what we give our other sitter?"

I nodded. What a relief he hadn't asked my rates. He showed me the dog's schedule and gave me a key. Father George tootled toward me with the smooth-haired

Chihuahua in his arms, smiling when the dog's whine changed to a growl. *If it hisses like a snake, it bites like a snake.* No worries, Mom. He'll be good when it's time to eat.

Back at my apartment, Sparky jumped onto the phone table. One ring, two rings. What alerted him that the phone would ring?

"Garrison residence, Cookie speaking."

"Any pet sitting jobs yet?" asked Polly.

"Walking a fun dog named Og. He lives on the first floor."

"Cute. Anything else?"

"Watching a Chihuahua. This will keep me busy. It's exciting."

"Please call another pet sitter. Her name is Louise Lester. Got a pencil?"

"Yes, but why?"

"She had to quit because of problems. You need to talk to her."

That didn't mean anything bad would happen to me. "You and Sparky fret too much."

"What's he doing?"

"Yowling a lot. Must be jealous."

"Cats have a sixth sense about future trouble. Be cautious with the Chihuahua. Even though they're small, some are mean. My sister's neurotic pooch attacked a horse."

Before I hung up, I wrote down Louise Lester's number on a scrap of paper and laid it on the counter. Any breed of dog can be mean or sweet, depending on its training and care. I hoped Fluffy would become friendlier soon.

When I walked inside my apartment, Sparky brushed against my leg. "Treat? Treat?" I asked.

He darted to the hall closet to paw his bag of treats. After he ate a couple, he tossed a catnip contraption into the air. I laughed out loud at his enthusiasm. The toy used to be his favorite, but his latest thrill was to hide hair bands under the bathroom rug. If I left to pet sit, he'd be alone more, but he slept most of the day and ate free choice food. He'd be okay.

"Be back after I take out the trash," I said, dragging a red sack into the hall to shove into a large chute. This new building had an extravagant disposal and recycling system. Junk slid down a black trough to drop into a basement container, then be sorted according to the bag color. When I lifted the opening, my nose whiffed spoiled food. The stench downstairs must be overpowering.

Back at the Anderson's house, Fluffy spotted me through a window, then scurried under a storage building. Uh-oh. That, I hadn't anticipated. In the yard, I called, "Fluffy, come. Supper. Eat. Come."

When he didn't obey any of my commands, I settled into a lawn chair and set his food bowl beside me, sure he'd return soon. An hour later, I realized my choices were to spend the night in the yard or come up with an alternate strategy. There were no dog treats in the kitchen or in any of the closets. After thirty minutes, I stopped the search and drove home to find something to tempt that ridiculous dog. Yes! In my fridge, there was a container of cooked meat. No dog could resist that.

When the dog saw me again, he scampered back to his hideout. The hamburger smell tickled my nose as I made a trail of pieces from the shed. The Chihuahua ate each one and then crawled under the building. I sighed. That wasn't a stellar plan. What now?

A nearby squeak startled me. Officer Bob Hope had opened the gate; he and his partner walked toward me. Nuts! Why didn't these guys quit harassing me?

Officer Bob spoke first. "Well, it's Cookie. Looks like you're in trouble again."

"I'm trying to bring the dog inside," I explained.

"Neighbors dialed 9-1-1, said you're stealing a Chihuahua."

The 9-1-1 dispatchers must be busy this month. "That's absurd. You know I'm a pet sitter."

"Don't argue," advised Bob. "Let's see your driver's license."

I bit my bottom lip to keep from asking why. Bob insinuated again that I meant to take Fluffy. The officers looked at my license for the second time, along with a note the dog's owner had left.

The hairs on my neck prickled. I rolled my lips together to lock my mouth and not say anything that might irritate the policemen. After a pause, I released my tongue from the roof of my mouth. "The owner's son called me. Their regular sitter is ill. The dog doesn't know me yet. You can contact Mr. Anderson for verification."

"Sorry," whispered Officer Tom. "He's a little over-enthusiastic."

More than a little. After the two departed, I propped the door open to make a line of hamburger from inside the house toward the shed. I hid behind the door until Fluffy scooted inside, then blocked his exit. Exhausted, I collapsed into the recliner. Within seconds, the dog landed in my lap and licked my nose. Then he jumped off and scurried down the hall for a squeaky ball. After four tweets, he dropped it in front of me.

When we both grabbed for it at the same time, his teeth dug into my skin. "Ouch. That stung." I stared at the sliced hand. Blood oozed from it and dripped onto the floor. I hastened to the bathroom to clean the punctures. The medicine cabinet had an antibiotic lotion but no bandages. I smeared a glob of Petroleum jelly on it, then remembered my first aid kit was in the car. Finally, I stopped the heavy bleeding with a wide band-aid. Darn. Dark drops of blood dotted the hall floor, bathroom, and Fluffy.

It wasn't funny, but I laughed. "You've got the measles. I'm tired – will clean up this mess tomorrow."

When I locked the door, the Chihuahua yapped and scratched at it. Although my muscles, my head, and my hand hurt, I forced myself to shop for dog treats. The elder Mr. Anderson might not approve of people food for Fluffy, and I didn't intend to spend more money on that dog.

That night, I posted reminders on my bulletin board:
    1. Keep pet treats in the car.
    2. Ask type and ages of pets.
    3. Keep a first-aid kit handy.

Could pet sitting become overwhelming or even dangerous? How many more injuries before I had a serious one?

CHAPTER EIGHT

ADHD BULL TERRIER

It was dark when I arrived at my apartment. "Sparky, it's almost ten o'clock, but we'd better listen to our calls."

My boy tipped his head and stared at me. "Meow." If he could talk, he'd say, "Why bother with that?"

There were two messages – a schedule update from Nick Anderson and a potential customer's request. That client was an apartment resident. His voice mail said, "This is Ben Young. We need to hire someone to feed and walk our bull terrier, Max. Eunice Taylor recommended you. We live on the fourth floor."

It was too late to respond to either message; besides, I was exhausted.

Sunday morning, I awoke rested, keen to tackle the day. As I drove to the Anderson's house, pet sitting questions confused my brain. Should I take another dog assignment? Og was ideal, but not Fluffy. With him, I'd netted injuries, minimal money, and huge stress. If I continued with pet sitting, I must become better acquainted with potential clients and their pets.

Fluffy watched me freshen his water and add kibble to the food dish. Most of his spots were gone – his measles case was now a light one. We played ball until I opened the door and handed him a rawhide treat. He took it, slipped outside, and disappeared under the storage building. With an assortment of cleaning supplies, I eliminated the blood remains on the hall floor and in the bathroom. I hoped a Fluffy bath wasn't necessary but would be prepared on the next visit. Yuck! That meant another expense for dog shampoo.

At home, Sparky sniffed Fluffy on my clothes and purred in my ear. I dialed Ben Young, Max's owners. When Ben Young answered, the cat yowled, jumped down, and left the room.

"What's that?" asked Ben.

"My cat. This is Cookie Garrison. Is this afternoon okay to meet Max? I'll be home from church around noon."

Sunday had been Carl's and my special day. At church, we snacked in the hospitality area where sumptuous tiny cheesecakes, Krispy Creme donuts, and flavored coffee welcomed worshipers. Then we joined our Bible study class before going to the main service.

But, after Carl died, church was not a comfortable place. Folks tried to help me but didn't know what to say or do. It was better now, but in the sanctuary, I still imagined sitting with Carl in the third pew.

At one o'clock, I boarded the elevator to go to the fourth floor. Ben Young opened the door and said, "Welcome. Have a seat. I'll get Max."

Ben and his wife, Evelyn, were probably in their thirties, a good-looking couple with a lovely apartment, complete with oak furniture and a massive leather sofa. Oversized animal photographs adorned the walls.

When Ben unlocked the crate, the bull terrier raced out of it and brought a stuffed pink elephant to me. Before I got it, he grabbed the toy and raced around in circles. *Be careful. You'll get hurt again.* Mom, I don't need your advice.

After Max thundered into the kitchen for a drink of water, I tossed his elephant into the center of the room. He retrieved it raced down the hall and back. Wow. He'd be a star poster dog for Ritalin. The white dog's pointed mouth, egg-shaped head, and pricked ears accented his triangular eyes to give him a scary appearance. Perhaps he was too strong and active for me.

Evelyn laughed. "He's crate-trained and responds to treats, but, off lead, he'll run off. Have you ever cared for a bull terrier?"

"No, but I can give you references."

"We don't need them. Eunice told us you're wonderful with Og."

Ben asked if I'd take the job. Hmm. I watched Max tearing around the apartment but noted he was friendly. Maybe he had so much excessive energy because he'd been crated. I hesitated but agreed, rationalizing it would only be for three days.

As I descended the stairs to my floor, I pondered my pet sits so far. It might be advisable to call Louise Lester, the pet sitter. However, I couldn't because the phone number had vanished, and I didn't want to pester Polly to get it again.

At midnight, a vivid vision woke me. In it, my mouth wouldn't open. When did I have my last tetanus vaccination? Though my injury, caused by Fluffy, wasn't serious, I couldn't get back to sleep. It took fifteen minutes to find my shot records. Hurray! The last vaccination wasn't that long ago – no danger of lockjaw. Why did I worry about such stuff?

I was asleep before the clock struck one, but at six, forced myself to awaken. Still tired, I admired the photos on the wall across the room. They were from my trips with Olivia – the New Mexico balloon festival and an Alaskan cruise.

"What are your plans now?" had been a frequent question at my retirement party. My answer was "travel." But, at that time, there were too many people and a dog who needed my care. When Olivia completed her book, we'd take another trip.

I checked my new e-mails before visiting Fluffy. The first one said:

> My name is Geneva Delbert. Aunt Eunice recommended you to pet sit. My husband and I live in St. Louis, but we'll pay extra for travel if you stay a week beginning May 3. Please respond yes or no. What are your rates?

Was it too soon to take on an out-of-town job? I'd have to refuse anything in Springfield and figure out what to charge. I wanted the experience but wasn't sure Polly should watch Sparky for a week. She had enough concerns.

I logged onto the Internet to seek information on typical costs. Too expensive, the family might hire a local sitter. Too little, they might question my competence. After deciding on an amount, I responded with a "yes," gasping when my pinkie hit the enter key. The letters in the address said, "gobs of pets." Darn. How many was that? What about snakes? What about iguanas? Had I made a big mistake?

The phone interrupted my confusion. "Will you be at lunch bunch today?" asked Olivia.

"No – have lots to do."

"Have you made any decisions about your life?"

"Yes. Pet sitting it is, even if you don't approve."

"Why say that? I'm not judgmental."

"You don't have pets, and you have always avoided mine."

"I'm allergic to cats. Don't you remember my dog, Bear?"

Poor Bear. The humongous German shepherd chased a squirrel into the road, and a car mashed the dog. Before that, Olivia's husband died of cancer. Hmm? A pattern? Dead mate – no more relationships; dead dog – no more pets. She had horrible losses, too, just at a younger age than me.

Olivia spoke louder. "It's your life. Do whatever delights you. Is anything else appealing?"

"Travel. I'm ready for another vacation."

"My book will be published by fall. Let's pick dates. Any other plans?"

"Might attend some Nature Center programs. There's one Thursday about Missouri owls."

"Include me. What time?"

Huh? What? Except for lunch outings and travel, Olivia never joined me, but perhaps I hadn't invited her enough times. Sometimes I'm too self-centered. What about that, Mom? No response.

That night, I was asleep before ten but didn't wake up until a loud commotion outside jarred me. Anxious to read another e-mail from Geneva, I booted up my computer. Her response said:

```
Excited to have you care for our animals.
Your price is fair. I'll send you particulars.
We're not leaving until afternoon. Plan to be
here by 1:00 p.m. Thanks.
```

I added to my growing reminders list:
1. Keep treats in the car.
2. Ask the type and age of pets.
3. Health problems, ages, unusual habits.
4. Medical records/meds.
5. Local, vet, and emergency contact info.
6. Don't lose your first-aid kit.
7. Visit the home and pets. Uncomfortable, say no!

A thought erupted. I'd accepted an assignment in a far-away city without knowing much. There wasn't enough information to judge if that was excellent, unpleasant, or neither.

"Sparky, what misfortunes can happen in St. Louis? Guess one of the pets can die, but I'll buy liability insurance. Or I might be miserable, but it's only a week. If I die from a snake bite, you'd be homeless, but someone would take you."

Sparky yowled four times as if to say, "No, no, don't go."

Of course, none of those bad things happened, but I failed to anticipate what did.

CHAPTER NINE

VISITING WINNIE

Most Tuesdays, I volunteered where my mother had spent her last days. For several months, when I entered the Oaks Nursing Home, tears formed in my eyes. But I learned to replace sad memories with wonderful ones – fun, exciting adventures along with many quiet times with Mom. In the hallway, a sharp odor of urine and chemicals made me sneeze. An oxygen machine gurgled, and, at the nurse's station, loud beeps indicated a resident had a problem. Can't let my pet sitting interfere too often with my visits here.

In the storage room, I put on an apron before traveling from room to room with a cart of juice, soda, and snacks. Few of the residents knew my name, but most of the long-time ones recognized me. The staff had presented me with a button that said: "Drink Lady."

I finished my duties, then found Mom's roommate, Winnie, in her room. The ninety-year-old lady had no living relatives and infrequent visitors. Although the Oaks' staff encouraged her to participate in activities, the caregivers were seldom successful, but Winnie did appreciate my visits.

She sat in her wheelchair in front of a blaring television, asleep. But after a few minutes, she shouted, "Where have you been?"

As I grasped the feeble hands, I imagined Mom's twisted ones, bent from arthritis. Those younger than me marveled that my mother lived to be ninety-one, but, after watching what some people endured, I might prefer the alternative.

On warm days, the staff permitted me to push Winnie's wheelchair into the courtyard. Sometimes she could barely move, but that day was better than most. I took a sweater from the minuscule closet and moved her arms into the sleeves. When we arrived at an exit, a nurse nodded, the signal she had unlocked the door.

Squirrels scampered in the trees, and birds tweeted to each other. We had been in the courtyard many times but seldom saw anyone else. Perhaps friends and relatives of residents were too busy to bring them there. Winnie moaned about her delusions and the rest home food. Instead of hearing her incessant chatter, my thoughts turned to potential items to buy for the St. Louis trip.

After a while, my old friend poked my arm with her finger. "Are you listening? It's my nap time."

We passed through the entry where an aide took Winnie to her room. From the nursing home, I went to the Anderson's house to exchange the key for my pay. When Nick asked if there had been any problems with Fluffy, I hesitated. No use to mention that the dog hid under the shed or that we had a collision with his teeth. I said, "Uh, nothing I couldn't handle. Fluffy got used to me."

Nick thanked me and smiled, but his father had a grumpy look, not pleased with my answer. On the way home, I stopped at Walmart to get a travel toothbrush and a few snacks. In the book racks, I located a St. Louis travel guide and the newest Janet Evanovich novel. Next, I priced cell phones. Polly had suggested I buy one with no required contract – just a fee for time each month. The clerk explained my options and helped me with setup. That was the best item I had purchased in weeks.

Before walking the bull terrier, I read my e-mails and listened to phone messages. First, I opened Geneva Delbert's e-mail. It contained explicit directions to the St. Louis house but no other information. Darn, still didn't know what pets the family had, but I had committed to do the job even if I had to feed snakes. Yuck! I shuddered, attempting to erase the vision of a snake swallowing live mice.

Daughter Marsha had news about my grandchildren and frustrations with four students in her third-grade class. Olivia offered me a ride to the Nature Center owl program on Thursday. Fiddlesticks! That had slipped my mind.

When the e-mail responses were sent, I made two phone calls. Marge answered on the first ring. "Sorry I haven't called you," I said. "I've been really busy."

"There's a dance this Friday at the Elks Club. Let's go. You can wear that red blouse."

"Uh, sorry. I'm leaving town soon." A dance with Marge and her friends – no way!

Next message was from Nora. When she didn't pick up, I responded on her answering machine – glad the fussbudget wasn't home.

On the way to the kitchen, I glanced into the cat's box. A scrap of paper with Louise Lester's phone number rested between a pile of toy mice. I stomped my foot and yelled, but Sparky had eaten plastic, rubber bands, and paper in the past. It was my fault for leaving the scrap where he could find it. While he settled into my lap to forgive my temper tantrum, I punched the pet sitter's number. A squeaky voice answered.

"My name's Cookie Garrison," I said. "A friend told me you used to be a pet sitter, but you quit."

"I don't recommend it to anyone. During the first month, a dog bit me, and a cat died. The second month, my car was stolen with a vicious dog in it. The owner sued me." Louise continued her grumbles about an ancient cat, snakes, and more.

"Uh, someone's here. Bye." *Don't lie. Your tongue will fall out.* Mom. It will not.

"Wait. That's not all," insisted the pet sitter.

Enough of that nut! I slammed the phone onto the table and stuffed Max's key into the pocket of my red windbreaker, confident he'd be easier to manage than Fluffy.

As they often are, my conclusions were wrong.

CHAPTER TEN

NOSY NORA

When I stepped into the hall, I shuddered. Nosy Nora was by the elevator, waving and yelling my name. She hurried toward me and tried to step inside my apartment, but I managed to push her away and lock the door.

"Why are you here?" I asked.

"You weren't at lunch bunch – thought you were sick."

Each moment my frustration increased. I wanted to yell at her. "Do I ever report to you when I'm busy? I'm off to walk a dog."

She pursed her lips and twisted her mouth, her way of expressing disgust. "I'll wait in your apartment until you can brew tea."

No way. A pet-hating person, she despised cats. Fred might hide, but Nora would snoop in all my drawers. I ran down the hallway to the elevator, hoping to shut her out, but wasn't fast enough. As it closed, she pushed her foot inside and joined me.

I said, "This is a locked building. Who let you in?"

"Told a guy I forgot my key. Why are you walking a dog?"

I wanted to lie but had made a resolution not to do that ever again. "I'm pet sitting a bull terrier."

"That's not safe. The lunch bunch gals told you no job."

Why did friends stress about my safety? I glued my mouth closed. No need to argue.

The elevator clunked as the door opened onto the fourth floor. With my stern teacher frown, I ordered Nora to stay there until I came back.

Max bounded out of his crate to race around the apartment. After four tries, I managed to hook a retractable leash to the dog's jeweled silver collar. He jumped and pulled, impatient to go outside. I shortened the lead and set the lock for better control, but he still dragged me down the hall. When Nora saw us, she hurried toward a sign marked "Stairs." Max and I rode the elevator to the first floor without her company.

The bull terrier tugged me out of the elevator and outside, toward the walking path that snaked into the woods. Sweat poured down my forehead, and my arms ached. When I yanked on the dog's lead, he jerked harder. The lock snapped, and yards of black leash flew behind him. A loud popping alerted me, and I gazed upward. Sliver metal, part of the hook, flew through the air toward my head. Although I jerked sideways, it wasn't fast enough to avoid the impact of the chunk of metal. Blood spots decorated my clothes as the dog charged into the woods. I had to capture him before he got lost or hit by a car. It had been a mistake to agree to care for the bull terrier.

Instead of leaving, Nora had plunked herself on a sidewalk bench to watch the confusion. I yelled at her, "Call Polly. Tell her I need aid with a dog." I pressed the windbreaker against my head wound to decrease the blood flow.

"You're bleeding. I'll dial 9-1-1."

"No. The chaos will scare the dog. Just call Polly! Please."

I continued down the path, my jacket sopped with blood. As the trees thickened, I saw an occasional squirrel scamper up a tree but no dog. I clapped and yelled over and over. "Max. Come."

Suddenly, the bull terrier circled my legs and grasped my jeans. I lunged to grip his collar but missed, and he galloped toward the apartment parking lot. My feet felt as if they were encased in lead, and fallen branches attacked me. Every inch of my body hurt, but on the bright side, my head no longer bled. Cringing, I staggered down the path, stumbling on roots and rocks until I fell to the ground. Maybe I'd just stay put for a while. No. A car might hit Max. Despite my pain, I forced myself to forge ahead. For support, I grasped an occasional tree, struggling to catch my breath. Then, above the commotion from the parking lot, I heard Polly call the dog.

As I exited the path, I witnessed a wonderful sight! My friend had kneeled to extend an open palm toward the bull terrier. He tipped his head, then trotted over to receive the treat she held in her palm. She took hold of the dog's collar to clip another leash to it. When she pointed to the ground, the dog downed and waited for her next command. Time for a new name for her – Pet Whisperer Polly.

Nora had called 9-1-1. Emergency personnel exited two fire trucks and an ambulance. Apartment residents gathered to gawk at the spectacle. More sirens announced other vehicles were on the way. Darn! The bloodhounds, Bob Hope and Tom Jones, had pulled up in their police cruiser. Officer Bob stuck his head out the window. His lower lip protruded, making him look like an unhappy Jack-o-lantern.

"Are you stealing that ugly dog?" he asked.

"Of course not," I answered. "He escaped, and he's not ugly."

The officer's facial expression mellowed. "You're bleeding."

I cringed and tried to joke. "At least the stains match my windbreaker."

He motioned at a medic. "We're leaving. He'll take care of you. Let's go, Jones. Nothing to do here."

A paramedic patched my aching head. "Let's get you in the ambulance. You need to be checked at the hospital."

"I'll be okay. The bleeding quit."

He shrugged. "Your choice. I can't force you, but you could have a concussion."

"I'll drive her to the urgent care center," said Polly.

Nora listened to our exchange. "What about me? Give me the apartment key. Guess I'll have to fix my own tea."

Polly glared at her. "Not today. Go home."

"Humph." Nora scurried toward her aging Ford, grumbling about inconsiderate people.

After we rode the elevator upstairs to crate Max, Polly drove me to urgent care. There, the doctor sewed stitches into my forehead and asked me a bunch of irritating questions. Where was I? What was the date?

Who was the President? What was my social security number?

"Why do you need that?" I asked. "I have a headache, but that's all."

He nodded, then cautioned me concerning the possible symptoms of a concussion.

On the way to the apartment, Polly asked, "Are you okay?"

"Yes, could've been worse. Thanks for catching Max."

"Why was Nora here?"

After I unlocked the apartment door, I reviewed the day's events while rolls baked and the coffee reheated. The pungent aroma of cinnamon filled the room as a tray of goodies slid from the oven. While I set them on the table, I looked at Polly. Bloodshot, puffy eyes, and pale skin had replaced her usual healthy appearance. I'd been too self-occupied to notice how miserable she looked.

"What's the matter?" I asked.

Tears streamed down her face. She blew her nose and tried to speak. "Albert, he…he wants a… a divorce."

Polly and Albert were a team – married for forty years. They had three adult children and five grandchildren. Sparky jumped onto her lap, meowing as if he understood her suffering.

She smiled and patted his head.

I placed a glass of water in front of her. "I'm so sorry. Why don't you stay here for a while? Maybe there's someone who could sub for me in St. Louis."

She took a sip before she spoke. "I doubt that. Thanks, but I have to confront Albert. Please, can we eat and not talk for a while?"

When her sobbing stopped, she said, "If you insist on pet sitting, please buy a cell phone."

"Already done that. Trying to figure out all the features. I'll write down the number for you."

Before she left, Polly offered me a hug and advised me to be careful. What on earth had happened to her marriage? Men! Maybe Albert had interest in a younger gal, but that was tough to imagine.

My head hurt, and I was woozy but had to feed Max. The dog crawled out of his crate, more sedate than before his escape. *There's good in most things, except ticks and mosquitoes.* Mom, enough. Go away.

After I refreshed the bull terrier's water and food dish, I turned on the radio. Ben Young claimed it calmed Max. The dog galloped into his crate and woofed twice for his Kong filled with peanut butter, a treat Ben had left for him.

The next day, I rose at six for a busy day of cleaning and shopping. Getting ready for a trip was fun, but not that day. Worries about Polly canceled the thrill of it. I added her number in my cell contacts and pushed the dial icon. "Trying out my new phone. Did you load mine into your contacts?"

"Sure did. Now, I'm going to work in the garden."

"I'll be gone a week. Are you sure you want to visit Sparky?"

"Yes. You know he's one of my favorite cats. Don't fret about me."

Her words encouraged, but she sounded shaky. Even when we're busy, we don't always have the will to do anything. Visiting Sparky would help her stay occupied.

After exercising Max, it was time for the owl program. Before Olivia arrived, I combed my hair over the stitches on my head.

The auditorium was packed, but we found two empty seats on the front row. A female volunteer from the Dickerson Park Zoo took a tiny screech owl from a small crate. The bird rested on the docent's hand while she discussed its habitat. The light brownish-red coloring had splotches of white and dark brown, and its yellow eyes stared into the audience. When the owl trilled, the docent asked, "Anyone have a mouse?" The crowd exploded in laughter. She deposited the owl in a cage with a blue cloth over it. "The screech owl is afraid of the bigger breeds. In the wild, they might eat her."

In the second cage, a light-colored barn owl perched on a limb. His striking plumage glistened, and the heart-shaped face froze until the presenter lifted him. Then, he extended his magnificent wings and made a spine-chilling hiss.

The great horned was next. The volunteer's gloved hand reached for the large fellow as we admired his distinctive feathered tufts, which resembled ears and were part of the owl's camouflage. A farmer had removed the female from a field before the bird's parents could teach her how to hoot. Now the huge bird made a squeaking sound instead.

Zoo personnel hoped to rehabilitate all injured animals, but, according to the docent, these three would die if released into the wild. She advised, "If you see a young owl on the ground, don't pick it up. His parents will take care of him."

After the demonstration, the audience members filed into the woods, where a guide played recorded owl calls. A great horned responded with "who, who, whooo, whooo," and swooped into a tall oak tree. No one spoke as the creature preened her feathers before she flew into the night sky.

"Fabulous program," said Olivia. "Glad you invited me. I never thought of all the dangers for owls. If you don't enjoy pet sitting, consider being a zoo docent. The schedule said there's an upcoming program about hummingbirds."

"I just about canceled tonight but glad I didn't."

"Is that because you're going to St. Louis?"

"When did you see Polly?"

"Yesterday, at the bank."

"Did she gossip about my bull terrier accident?"

"Yep. You don't have enough hair to hide those stitches."

I pulled at my hair and forced a frown. "That's cruel."

"Why didn't you mention the St. Louis trip? If you're worried about my approval, don't. When will you be back?"

"In a week. Did Polly seem all right to you?"

"I guess. Why?"

"Just wondered." Not my place to mention Polly's problems.

"You're perkier today. If pet sitting doesn't pan out, regroup and do something else. Whatever you choose, your mistakes don't define you, but you can learn from them."

I smiled. Olivia always had sage opinions.

On Friday morning, Max's owner called to say they were back. Reluctantly, I trudged upstairs to explain about the broken leash, expecting them to be angry. Instead, I received an apology and a check with a ten-dollar tip. As I opened the door to leave, I heard Ben say to his wife, "That's the third lead he's broken."

I learned pet owners won't always inform me about the worst, or perhaps they hope it doesn't happen.

CHAPTER ELEVEN
POLLY'S GIRLS

Polly plopped into her recliner. She wasn't at all okay, but she didn't want Cookie to worry. Her body felt strange – chilled and shaky. Why hadn't she tried harder to encourage her friend to refuse the St. Louis assignment? It was not an opportune time for Cookie to travel anywhere, especially to an unfamiliar location. Premonitions were seldom wrong.

At the least, she might have insisted Cookie contact the pet sitter, Louise Lester. Though the woman was strange, she had been a full-time pet sitter. Polly met the gal at a therapy dog meeting in February, where Louise tried to qualify her Schnauzer, Misty, for visits at local schools. Unfortunately, the dog was skittish, afraid of the distractions, and hesitant to leave her owner. It could not be certified.

Before the trials began, Louise complained about the perils of pet sitting. At the time, it occurred to Polly that the woman was an irresponsible flake, but the experienced pet sitter did relate some legitimate concerns.

Polly watched her own aging pet therapy dog, Peeka, curl onto a dog bed. The twelve-year-old English setter had been retired from her weekly visits to the children's wing of the hospital. Penelope, the new pup, was enrolled in a puppy socialization class. Her next one would be Home Manners. Polly hoped the mutt would take Peeka's place when she was old enough, but she had to pass the pet therapy dog test first. Polly lifted the puppy into her arms just as the phone rang.

"Hi. This is Roger. Is Albert there?"

"Uh, not now. May I give him a message?"

"Hunting a fourth for golf. I'll try someone else. Tell him I called."

Albert snoozed in the guest room, but Polly wouldn't let his buddy know her husband was still in bed. No way she'd let Albert ruin her day. She had flowers to plant and Penelope's daily training to do, but then she remembered her daughters planned to take her to lunch. Although an outing with them was delightful, she dreaded their questions about their father. They hadn't seen him in two weeks.

At ten, Alicia arrived. "Where's the new pup?"

"Shut in the kitchen. She's not house trained yet. Go get her."

Alicia's flowing skirt swirled, and her auburn braids swayed as she tried to hold onto the wiggly pup. She sat down on the living room floor, mashing the skirt underneath her. Penelope raced around as Alicia waved a rope toy at the pup.

Polly smiled at the two and found Alicia a ball. "Take her out back. See if you can teach her to fetch."

"Okay. Yell when Liz gets here."

Thirty minutes later, the youngest in the family bounded into the room. She wore torn jeans and a sweatshirt. No use to urge her to dress more appropriately. Liz didn't listen to her mother's objections about that or anything else.

"Alicia's in the yard," Polly said. "Ask her to crate Penelope."

"Where's Dad?" asked Liz.

Polly pretended to search the closet for a sweater. "Uh, not sure – maybe golfing."

Liz scowled and bit her bottom lip. "Why is he never home?"

"It's a coincidence. Let's have lunch at the Sunrise Tea Room. Cookie recommended it."

At the restaurant, the three located an empty table where they could see the garden. Polly placed her purse on an extra chair and put a rabbit's foot on top of it. She believed better luck with money occurred if one's billfold never touched the floor. They all ordered the daily special, half a grilled cheese sandwich with potato soup. While they drank their iced tea, they admired the garden courtyard. The two sisters chatted while Polly stared through the window.

"Alicia to Mom. Where are you?"

"Sorry. Just reflecting about life."

"Time to fess up. Why is Dad never home? Where is he?"

Polly sighed. "I'd rather not say."

Liz chimed in, "We'd rather you did. If you don't, we'll invade your house until we see him."

Alicia frowned at her sister but said nothing because, at that moment, the waitress brought their food.

"Later. Let's have a civil conversation while we eat," said Polly.

As they ate, Liz praised one of her college instructors, and Alicia, a teacher, complained about her first-grade class. Polly stared at the garden without comments.

After the waitress collected the empty plates, she took dessert orders. Both girls ordered Polly's favorite, cheesecake with fresh strawberries, but their mother declined to order.

"No dessert?" said Liz. "What's the matter with you?"

Polly took a deep breath to prepare what she had to tell her girls. "Albert wants a divorce."

"What? You've been married forever," said Alicia. "Why?"

"That's the…"

Polly interrupted Liz. "Don't say it. I don't appreciate your vulgar language."

"That's the…the pits."

"Girls, don't hover. Don't call. I'm all right." *Even though I can't eat or sleep.*

Alicia said, "We'll stay out of your way until…"

"Next Saturday," interrupted Liz. "Then we're interrogating Dad. In the meantime, let's plan a yard sale."

"What? No way," said Polly.

Alicia said to Liz, "Can't believe you changed the subject to a garage sale. But I do have a bunch of stuff to dump."

"Girls, never again. That's a lot of extra work."

"Come on," said Liz. "You need distractions from your worries. Let's dig out boxes and clean closets. I can use the extra money."

"Me too," said Alicia. "I have kids' clothes, toys, and old kitchen stuff. This is the best season for a sale. Last year I bought an attractive new outfit with my profits."

Polly pointed at Liz. "Last year, after your vast promises, you didn't show up on sale days."

"I'm the oldest sibling and the most responsible," said Alicia. "I won't let you down. Cookie can come. We had fun at her moving sale."

"She's busy pet sitting," said Polly.

"Since when?" asked Liz.

"A few days ago. She's in St. Louis now. I'm worried. Her horoscope is scary. This morning I saw another apprehension of evil. There was an owl in that big maple tree. When seen in the daytime, that's a sign of bad luck."

Neither girl spoke. Based on their observations since childhood, they both knew Polly had a sixth sense, especially about upcoming dangers to self, family, or friends.

"Girls, I do not want any more talk about garage sales. Got it?"

Alicia nodded, but Liz avoided eye contact with her sister and mother. She was anxious to have a sale. Maybe she'd visit Cookie when their friend got back from St. Louis.

CHAPTER TWELVE

GOBS OF PETS

As I lifted a suitcase from the closet shelf, Sparky yowled. I threw him a new catnip toy, but he'd have nothing to do with it. When I picked him up, he responded with a cat hug. "It's okay, fellow. Polly will visit while I'm gone."

After I loaded luggage into the Buick, I surfed Internet sites for insurance information. If I joined a pet sitting association, liability coverage and other perks were included. It was expensive, but maybe I needed it. So far, my track record was mediocre. Although no one had criticized me, that could change, especially if something terrible occurred.

"Hey, Sparky, why don't people check my background? When I say I'm a retired teacher, they assume I'm a competent pet sitter. Most teachers, ministers, nurses, and others are trustworthy, but as Mom often said, 'There's a rotten apple on every tree.'"

The cat tilted his head and meowed.

The Gobs of Pets Caper

"Never mind. It's not a real apple."

I lined up toy mice, hair bands, and cloth balls on the coffee table for Sparky to play with in my absence. After filling his self-feeder, I placed treats beside it, then swiped away tears, knowing he'd complain when I left. Silly to be so sentimental about a cat, even though he was a marvelous one.

Hurrying out the door, I told myself to relax, but uneasiness settled over me as I drove onto the Interstate, recalling my prior disasters on I-44. During the first one, a tire blew on the way to a teaching conference and hemmed my car between two semi-trucks. The second one took my husband's life. Polly often said bad events occurred in threes. I'm not superstitious, but....

When I reached Marshfield, my uneasiness left. Bradford pear and Redbud trees dotted the hillsides. At exit 161, I noticed a Cracker Barrel sign and slowed down. An hour later, full of eggs and pancakes, I walked out of the restaurant with a three-foot statue of a yellow Labrador, a duplicate of my long-gone canine pet, Frosty. Sometimes, I can't resist an exciting sale item.

Road signs to announce Rolla exits brought back vivid memories of my dead husband and his mashed Jeep. I shuddered as my car neared the spot where a drunk driver killed Carl. I sped over rolling hills to escape the terrible memories of that week.

A little over two hundred miles past Springfield, I reread the directions to Prince Lane. It was a wide street with majestic homes and impressive yards. I spotted Delbert's address on the mailbox of an enormous red-brick house. Wow! There was a large porch on the east end and a three-car garage on the west. Several trees and attractive bushes grew in the front yard with budding tulips brightening a circular flower bed beside the driveway. That was even a nicer place than my first pet sit with the Lab, Henry.

Early, I drove around for a while before strolling up to the ten-foot oak door with animals carved into it. In the middle, I lifted a knocker in the shape of a dog. A plump, buxom woman, probably in her mid-forties, greeted me with a cheery smile. Behind her, two black dogs barked and wagged their tails. Geneva commanded them to sit. The adult obeyed, but the puppy yapped and raced around the room. His owner caught the dog and put him in my arms.

"Welcome. Glad you're here. This is Thor, Thurber's offspring. He's a Labradoodle, has the gentle Lab temperament, and doesn't shed. Have a seat, and I'll pour you a drink."

I carried Thor to a shiny tan leather chair. The puppy licked my arm as I rubbed his curly, soft fur. Soon the little fellow fell asleep in my lap. Geneva put a tall glass of iced cola on an end table, then replaced the puppy with a thick notebook.

"Here are directions for our darlings. There are detailed information sheets with schedules for each animal. Morning chores are completed for today except for the old dog, Thomas. Take him out in a couple of hours. Do the evening duties around four. Read my notes while we pack the car."

I wondered if the notebook was rigmarole to impress me, but after reading the information in the front, I doubted that. It said:

DOGS; Thomas, Thurber, Thor
CATS: Alabama, Florida, Texas, Nevada
CHINCHILLAS: Jack, Jill
BIRDS: Percy, Peter, Paula, Petunia, Pam
RAT: Lucky
GOAT: Batman

The book had twenty pages of instructions with comments about each animal's needs and habits. No way I'd be able to explore the city that week. Darn! I still didn't have liability insurance.

Loud laughter bounced off the hallway walls. Geneva and a man entered the living room. The husband, John, introduced himself and extended his hand. Oily black hair stuck out from under a Royal's baseball cap, and round glasses teetered on his beaky nose. No specific reason, but I didn't trust him. He resembled a thug TV actor whose name I couldn't recall.

Geneva said, "Let's take a quick house tour." She motioned to the nearby room. "Of course, that's the kitchen. Eat whatever you can find. Now, the upstairs."

I put down the notebook and followed her. We viewed three bedrooms, each with antique furniture constructed of cherry or walnut wood. In an office, books overflowed on tall bookcases that stretched from floor to ceiling. Three of the rooms were painted mauve, but in one, wallpaper with pictures of dogs covered most wall surfaces.

As we walked, Geneva babbled about her various possessions and unusual art pieces. "Keep the upstairs doors shut. The animals and their supplies are all on the first floor. Next, we'll go downstairs."

There, we came to another bedroom, crowded with a gigantic four-poster bed and maple furniture. "At night, Thomas will stay here in his crate. The other two dogs can sleep with you," said Geneva.

The Gobs of Pets Caper

When we entered the sunroom, I gasped. Glass panels encased it with the sun creating streaks of shadows and light. The plethora of sights and sounds overwhelmed me. In a six-foot-tall aviary Percy, the macaw, greeted us with loud squawks. The African gray parrots, Peter and Paula, rested in their cage beside the home of a pair of cockatiels. I wrinkled my nose at the essence of musty old books. Cleaning these cages and feeding all the animals would require many hours a day.

Geneva removed the white rat from her cage. "Let down the blinds if it's too hot. You can hold Lucky and give her ear scratches, but she hates the cats." The rat squeaked as she skittered around her owner's neck.

"The macaw prefers women, but don't let him out. He might learn your name if you say it often." The bird extended his massive wings. "Hello, pretty boy. Percy's cool." Geneva reached inside the bird's home to touch him. "He's smart, but we're in a hurry. No time for tricks until we get back."

Twenty minutes later, we entered a small porch area with three litter boxes and several carpeted cat towers. The porch wrapped around the rear of the house, where a seven-foot privacy fence enclosed an oversized yard.

"We keep the gate padlocked," said Geneva. "The dogs can stay in the yard when you're here. If you leave, be sure to crate them, but do not forget the old dog has to potty frequently." She whistled, and a small goat trotted over to greet us. He had black hair with white around his nose and chest. A white triangle of fur on the top of his head accented his ears which stuck out, pointing upward. Geneva took a carrot from her pocket and scratched the goat's head. "Batman's no trouble, but he might escape if the gate's left open."

The animal wasn't over two feet tall. "Is he a pigmy?" I asked.

"No, we only acquire the best. He's a Nigerian dwarf goat with an impressive pedigree." She motioned toward the back of the property. In the mornings, give him hay from that storage shed. His grain is there in a metal container. Feeding instructions are in the notebook."

During the tour, I realized the importance of liability insurance. What if I spilled grape juice on someone's carpet? How would one explain a goat had eaten the neighbor's prized flowers? What if I stained a table or ripped a curtain? Worse, lost a pet.

"Do you have questions?" asked Geneva.

"None now, but I don't know much about goats."

"You'll do okay. Read the notebook info. Jot down any questions, even if they seem silly. I'll call you often. Oh, nearly forgot. In the basement, there's a recreation area with directions to operate the entertainment center."

After the Delbert's black Cadillac pulled onto the street, I called Polly. She answered after the first ring.

"I'm here," I said. "No snakes, but there are birds."

"What kind?"

"A scarlet macaw, a pair of African grays, and two cockatiels."

"That's unusual. Macaws and grays are rare and often quite expensive. Be leery. Parrots can bite. Anything else?"

"Cats, dogs, a goat, and a rat."

"Did you say goat? Can they have that in the city?"

"Guess so. His name is Batman. He's not very big."

"You didn't ask the appropriate questions. Watch for separation anxiety. Are the pets adapting to you?"

"The dogs are good. Haven't seen any cats yet. Anything new with Albert?"

"No. I don't want to discuss him. I'd better hang up."

I thought she needed to talk to someone, but that was her choice. Besides, I had enough to stress about for the next week.

The two active dogs followed me, watching as I unpacked, but sixteen-year-old Thomas stayed in his crate. When it was time to come out, he didn't budge. I crouched on the floor until he finally crawled out. He was about the size of a cocker with a pleasing but sad face and shaggy straw-colored hair. I carried him to the yard where Batman trotted over and butted my leg.

"You dogs, play. Batman, I'll get you a carrot."

After Thomas pottied, I carried the old guy inside and lifted him into his crate. He curled into a ball and moaned. As I watched the frail animal close his eyes, I recalled the time my mother said she was ready to die. Whether you are a dog or a human, the end of life can be a difficult journey.

Next, I read the evening chore information:
1. Feed Thurber and Thor.
2. Give Thomas his pills.
3. Scoop litter boxes and clean up outdoor poop.
4. Give Alabama runny nose medicine.
5. Take the dogs out, and play ball with Thor.
6. Check birdcages; replenish food as needed.
7. Give cats their evening meals.
8. Take Thomas out again right before bedtime.
9. Feed Batman grain.

Because Thomas didn't eat or drink late, he stayed in his crate all night, but at daylight, he'd have to go outside. According to the notebook, he might wake up to go out around 3:00 a.m. Darn! I hate to get up that early.

The Gobs of Pets Caper

That night it was after six before I finished most of the chores. The dogs watched me explore the kitchen cabinets and fridge for food. There were a few basics – ripe bananas, a loaf of bread, a jar of peanut butter, canned soup, and one sick-looking apple.

"Boys, tomorrow it's off to the grocery store. But tonight, I'll microwave a bowl of vegetable soup and a make PBJ, if there's jelly."

Thurber sat in front of me and barked.

"You guys had supper, but you can have a tiny bite of bread when I'm finished."

I left my soup and sandwich on the counter while I went to the bedroom for my Evanovich book. Just as I opened my suitcase, an explosive crash reverberated from the kitchen. I scurried back. Uh-oh. Pieces of carrots, beans, and pinkish liquid surrounded a bowl on the white tile floor. Thor licked up puddles of the mess while Thurber stretched his jaws open and shut. *You'd better get that insurance soon.* I will, Mom.

"Thurber, don't you know peanut butter sticks to your mouth?"

The Lab's tail drummed on the floor, flipping food onto furniture and cabinets. I sent the two dogs to the backyard while I cleaned up the massive spill. Thank goodness, there were no dents in the floor. I found another can of soup to heat in the microwave. When the last spoonful of soup entered my mouth, the landline phone jangled. It was Geneva, calling to check about her notes and ask a lot of questions.

Yes, the chores were done. Yes, I carried Thomas out. Yes, I locked up. After thirty minutes, she disconnected. I loaded the dishwasher and brought the dogs inside. Thor galloped into the kitchen, lost his footing, and slid on his bottom across the wet floor. I shook with laughter while Thurber barked at me.

"No treats. You had a whole sandwich. Let's go to sleep."

Too bushed to read my book, I tucked myself into the middle of the bed. Thurber leapt up beside me, and Thor whined to join us. After placing the pup on the end, I tucked myself under the silken pink sheets and pulled the comforter around my chin. Within fifteen minutes, two of the four cats jumped up, cuddling into the warmth of the comforter. I smiled at the menagerie of pet sounds, blended to create a peaceful, relaxing mood.

My eyelids grew heavy, but I had a sense of dread, thoughts of something evil lurking not far away. Nonsense. This was an upper-class, safe community. However, I found that conclusion had flaws.

Bad things happened before I had a chance to go online and pay the fee for insurance.

CHAPTER THIRTEEN

THE INTRUDER

The next morning, Thurber stood beside the bed staring at me. He pushed his nose under my arm. The clock on the nightstand said five-thirty.

"If we get up before sunrise, nine o'clock is our new bedtime. I need more rest."

After letting the Labs into the yard, I unhooked the old dog's crate to carry him outside. Batman and Thor chased each other while Thurber and Thomas rested near me on the porch.

"Are you too mature for a Thor-Batman game?" I asked Thurber. He whined and moaned. After fifteen minutes, I lugged Thomas into the kitchen for the old dog to lap a bowl of soft beefy food. Then, I held a water dish as he slurped the liquid before he curled into his fluffy dog bed.

Next, I traipsed to the sunroom to clean cages and feed the birds. Percy stared at me with vivid yellow eyes.

The scarlet macaw made a low-pitched squawk and a human-sounding scream. "Percy's cool."

"You're a loud fellow. Let's learn Cookie's cool, Cookie's cool."

The parrot cocked his head to one side but said nothing else. I replenished the birdseed and put fresh peeled apple slices in his empty dish. He plucked a chunk and nibbled on it with no more interest in me. The birthday song drifted from the cockatiels' cage, and the African gray parrots contributed to the sound riot.

My family never owned birds. When I was a preschooler, I wanted to buy a parakeet, but my father claimed they were too messy. When I don't have Sparky anymore, maybe I'll get a macaw. However, Polly said they are often illegally imported and quite expensive.

Time for the white rat. She resembled a pet my daughter bought when she was a teen. At first, I had hesitated to let Marsha keep the animal, but the rodent became a delightful member of our family. She rode on my daughter's shoulders, making happy sounds. Unfortunately, rats weren't good pets because they don't have lengthy life spans.

"Hi. Can you do tricks?" I asked.

Lucky chittered. When I reached inside the cage, she crawled up my arm. I lifted the rat off, scratched her head, and returned her home, then filled the food bowl.

"There you are, pretty girl. I'll bring you a treat later. Got to feed the chinchillas."

Jack and Jill each weighed around a pound. Their gorgeous thick fur and impressive ears made them look intelligent. Information in the notebook said, "Jack and Jill are tame, but leave them in their cage. Jill, the largest, is the female. They use a type of dust to clean themselves. It's fun to watch them roll in it. Wood chews are necessary because their teeth grow fast. For a treat, give them a new cardboard box and a few raisins."

When I finished the sunroom chores, I explored the entire house again. In the living room, I admired the complicated construction of a three-tiered chandelier. Each room had a different type of fixture, some with hundreds of glass bangles, others, less gaudy. In most of the rooms, enormous mirrors and paintings were crammed together, most with stunning gold frames. As I peered at the works of Picasso, Monet, and Van Gogh, I wondered how many were originals.

In the master bedroom, I fingered the colorful blue and yellow spread on a four-poster bed and admired statues of dogs, cats, and birds. I'm no antique expert, but much of the furniture and decorations were possibly Victorian. The contents of the home must be worth a fortune. On the way to the recreation room, my phone vibrated.

"Hi," said Polly. "How are you doing?"

"Won't be able to explore the city but don't mind the challenge. Although one old dog sleeps a lot, he's not in pain."

"How's the macaw? Did it try to bite?"

"He's gorgeous. The aviary is designed so he can't reach me. How are you doing?"

"Fair. I'm going to church today. Albert won't ruin my entire life. Is the house fancy?"

"Don't know I'd call it that. There's gobs of ornate furniture, paintings, and artwork."

"Don't break or spill anything. Did you order insurance yet?"

"No, but I will. How's Sparky?"

"He's fine, sits in my lap, and purrs. Better hang up since you're on a prepaid cell."

Pet Whisperer Polly didn't sound too upset. She'd work through the Albert situation, but with her psychic abilities, why didn't she know there was a problem with their relationship?

I searched the kitchen for more food but didn't find anything appealing. Thomas rested in his dog bed while I read the morning newspaper and ate some toast with grape jelly. Tired, I decided to take a nap.

Two hours later, I heard a loud banging noise outside. I forced my eyes open. It was the goat. Darn. I had forgotten to feed him. I took Thomas outside, where Thor, Thurber, and Batman greeted us. When the goat butted my arm, I went to the shed to pour grain into his food bucket.

"Here, fellow. Sorry I missed you, but you did have a carrot."

After Batman ate, I crated all the dogs, opened the garage, and drove onto the driveway. I had to wait until a medium-sized red delivery truck inched past the house and down the street. There was a dent in the passenger side and numerous paint scratches. It looked out of place in that upscale neighborhood. On the back, a sign said truck for rent with a southwest Missouri phone number. That seemed strange.

On the way to Schnucks grocery store, I admired the massive homes. They were more elaborate than the brown frame one where I had spent most of my life. But I treasured the pleasures shared there with Carl – raising a child together, laughing at the fun, and making up after disagreements. We had friendly neighbors, a beautiful park, and a small elementary school with lots of community involvement. When our AARP cards arrived, we discussed all the places we'd like to visit, starting with an Alaskan cruise. None of that happened. We knew everything about each other and were aware we'd both pass someday but never thought one of us would go so soon. I regretted what we'd wasted on idiotic stuff, not devoting time doing together things – bowling, traveling, playing cards, going to plays, visiting family, and so on.

Inside the store, I concentrated on reading my shopping list while pushing the grocery cart. While looking down, I didn't notice a male customer. Wham! I rammed the back of his legs.

He yelled, "Lady, watch out," scowling at me in a ferocious manner.

For a second, I thought he might hit me with his cart. I mumbled, "Oh, I'm so sorry."

He paused and smiled. Then his penetrating blue eyes softened. My face warmed under the weight of his stares. His previous sharp tone changed to a softer one with a playful lilt. "Do you carry insurance? Pretty women don't maul me often. My name is Brad Franklin, and you are...?"

"Uh, Casandra Garrison. People call me Cookie."

"Cute. Are you new in our neighborhood?"

He seemed harmless, but I don't share information with strangers. "I'm...I'm staying here for a few days." I needed to be polite since I attacked him but didn't know what else to say. I coughed then asked, "Do you live around here?"

He pointed toward the Delbert's subdivision. "Yes, over on Prince Lane."

Hmm. I admired the tall, muscular senior citizen as he talked about his community.

White streaks intruded his dark, wavy hair, and his mouth erupted into a dimpled grin. He resembled some movie star with the same first name, but who? My mind was blank.

"Enchanting lady," he said. "I'll buy you dinner. You can choose any restaurant."

No ring on his left finger. Although the invitation appealed to me, another relationship had all the charm of a yeast infection. Besides, the pet job at Delbert's kept me too busy to plan anything else.

Every muscle in my body tightened. "Uh, can't today."

"Give me your number so we can connect later. I bet you have a cell."

Of course, doesn't everybody nowadays? How would you know, Mom?

Why was this guy so insistent? "Thanks, but no. I'm busy," I said.

He tried to persuade me, but I hastened away to the shortest open checkout lane. There, I fidgeted because the elderly customer in front of me didn't have enough money for her groceries. Although gorgeous Brad didn't follow me, I wanted out of there.

I tapped the woman's back. "I'll pay the balance."

She was hesitant. "You're very generous, but..."

"You can do the same for someone else. Pay it forward."

In my car, I relived what had happened, not able to ignore the pleasant way Brad gazed at me. Why did someone as suave and attractive as him ask me to dinner? Maybe he thought we'd met before, but I knew we hadn't.

Forget him. You don't want another man in your life. I know, Mom, I need another relationship like an Eskimo needs a refrigerator. I must concentrate on buying insurance, worrying about Polly, and acting my age.

However, despite the fact I wasn't interested in the man, his attention caused a surge of elation through me. I hummed for the first time in many months.

From the garage, I toted six paper sacks of groceries inside and sat down to drink a glass of orange juice. Thurber perched beside my leg and pushed under my hand with his nose.

"You can't have – how did you? Can you unhook your crate, or didn't I lock it?"

The Gobs of Pets Caper

From somewhere in the house, there was a rumble, as if several large items had fallen off shelves. Then, closer, a window or door shut. Chills immobilized my body as I glanced around the room, telling myself all houses have their sounds – furnaces, pipes, pets. I hadn't noticed anything unusual in the garage. The racket must be in the front. I peeked out the door but saw no movement and heard no more noise. Then I felt another presence, not far away.

I stiffened at the sight of a powerful-looking giant looming in the kitchen doorway with Thor in his arms. He filled the opening, looking distinguished in a black suit with a shiny green tie. He wasn't fat, but his hefty build and height forced knots in my belly. Most men were taller than me, but this person had to duck at the doorway – must be close to seven feet.

The giant put Thor on the floor and picked up a duffle bag, then strode across the room to tower over me. He resembled a minister at a church I had attended more than five years ago. No way it was the same person, but was it? I couldn't forget such a huge man.

The dogs didn't fear the goliath figure. Could he be a friend or relative? Of course, a yummy treat would have made them buddies.

He pointed at a chair, "Sit down."

"Who are you?" I asked. *Don't irritate a robber until you know where his gun is.* Mom, he's not a robber — but I wasn't so sure.

He said, "Sit down, now!" His menacing sneer replaced his earlier pleasant expression. That alerted me that he must be an intruder. I squinted toward the counter where my cell rested, but when he saw that, he tossed the phone across the room. He removed a gun from the duffle and pointed it at me. "Who are you?" His dignified bass voice boomed as he moved closer, waving the gun back and forth. Would he shoot, or was it a meaningless threat?

As I scanned the room, my pulse raced, looking for something to use as a weapon. But an escape wouldn't work. The big guy could easily overpower me, then kill the dogs. Wonder if insurance would cover that? Both of them contently gnawed on new bones he must have brought.

Why didn't Thurber protect me? How did this giant know to bring dog treats? Had the dogs met him before? I willed myself to stop analyzing and quit shaking. I had to keep my mind clear and focused. I gazed at the floor, trying to think what to do.

"Look at me! What is your name?" said the gargantuan figure.

An icy feeling filled me like a freezer in the packing house where my father had stored meat. The man repeated his request with slow, precise enunciation. "Tell. Me. Your. Name."

I whispered my maiden name, "Cassandra Trent." Overwhelming terror gripped me. I felt light-headed, queasy. I shut my eyes to get control of my blurred vision.

"Miss Cas-san-dra, look at me! Perhaps I could lie and tell you I live here, but that isn't plausible, is it? This is the way it will be. You do not identify me in any way. Instead, you will create a convincing story to tell as many times as necessary. You will not call the police or the owners of this house until I am gone. If you don't do as I say, my friend and I will track you down. My partner has an interesting electrical device he tries on new victims. Or, if you prefer, I can demonstrate how to amputate a finger with my favorite tool. To summarize, a vile consequence will occur if you share anything about me with anyone. Do you believe me?"

My throat tightened, and my stomach told me I'd just drunk a can of Drano. Yelling, the monster repeated his question. Not able to speak, I nodded, shivering as he removed a piece of toweling from his duffle bag. He pressed his huge palm against my forehead to tilt my chin upward. Horrified, I felt a rag wrap around my nose and mouth. In seconds, the rag, room, and man faded.

Thoughts of torture rolled in my head until I lost all consciousness.

CHAPTER FOURTEEN

TOO MUCH DUCT TAPE

Was I dead? No, couldn't be. I just bought green bananas, and there's no pain in heaven, unless I was somewhere else. My head felt as if it had a metal band strapped around it. Silver duct tape attached my entire body to a chair while more of it cemented my mouth secure, and the rest of the roll wrapped around my feet. Wish the sinister minister had given me time to pee.

A chewing sound interrupted my efforts to loosen the restraints. Across the room, Thor gnawed on one of my favorite shoes. Thurber had one grocery sack on the floor and had knocked another over onto the counter. Darn. There were brownies in one of those. He'd be super sick or dead if he ate all of them.

I banged my feet on the floor to get the dogs' attention, but neither showed any interest in my predicament. Thor paid no mind, but Thurber galloped over, barked once, and then resumed his sack pursuit.

One more hit the floor just as the doorbell rang. The Lab yanked a loaf of bread from it and chased Thor to the entry. The dogs alternated between tearing the bread from the wrapper and barking. I rocked from side to side until the chair crashed to the floor. Still duct-taped, I couldn't get loose or open my mouth. But worst of all, I couldn't go pee.

My stomach clenched as the familiar click of a key alarmed me. Petrified, I feared it was the minister, but instead, it was the guy I had rammed at the grocery store. What was his name? Brad..., Brad Pitt? No, that was the actor from Springfield. Brad...something. Why was he here?

He halted at the door. "I called, but no one answered. What are you doing?"

What an idiotic question. I moaned, hummed, and thrashed until he pulled the chair upright and jerked the tape from my mouth.

"Ouch. That hurt. Cut me loose!" I demanded.

Instead of freeing my appendages, he called 9-1-1. My body ached. My tummy thought I had eaten a bucket of rocks, and I still needed to pee.

"Cut me loose!" I screamed.

"Hang on," said Brad. "Police are on the way. Why are the dogs eating bread?"

The Gobs of Pets Caper

I chose not to dignify the question with an answer, trying to remain calm while I waited for another rescuer. Maybe Brad "Something" would rethink his decision and decide to release me. *It could be worse.* No, Mom. You're wrong.

Police, paramedics, and firefighters stormed into the room. Emergency people must not have enough to do. Why firemen? Nothing burned except my face. At least those pesky police officers from Springfield weren't there.

Brad talked to a female officer, then left through the front door, but the room was still overflowing with people.

"Can't one of you cut this darn tape?" I yelled.

The female officer stepped around the breadcrumbs and dogs to point a camera at me. She snapped it twice and then took a knife from her pocket. After she freed my limbs, she pulled up a chair beside mine.

"I'm Detective Ruth Smart. I'll interview you, then the neighbor fellow."

"Please. I need to go pee."

The officer sighed. "Hurry. It's late, and my shift's nearly over."

After a bathroom trip, I shook my numb arms and stomped my feet. Thurber and Thor accompanied me to Thomas' crate, where the ancient fellow crawled out.

Several of my muscle groups screamed when I reached down to pick him up. Batman rushed over to me while the dogs wandered in the yard. I massaged my shoulders and neck as I rehearsed a logical story.

When I had all three dogs settled into their crates, I went back to Officer Smart. *Don't lie. One untruth will lead to another.* I'll be careful, Mom.

Officer Smart asked basic information about me, then inquired about the assailant. I moved my numb fingers and closed my eyes, knowing I must tell a believable story. First, the policewoman asked for a description of the intruder.

I shrugged. "Don't know. I didn't see him."

"What? The locks are broken, the gate's padlock cut, and there are tire tracks in the yard. What about his speech? What did you see? What did you hear? Are you sure it was a man?"

Uh-oh, didn't mean to say man. Relax. Get a grip. "I drove here from the market, unloaded groceries, and carried them inside. A person came behind me and held a cloth over my nose and mouth. When I woke up, they were gone, and I was taped to a chair."

"Are you positive that's all you know?"

When I nodded, she supplied me with paper and a pen. "Make a list of the missing items."

"I'm just the pet sitter – no idea what's gone."

Brad opened the front door and dashed over to us. He held a backpack and had an obvious bulge in his jeans pocket. "I'm on the sofa tonight in case Cookie needs protection," he told Officer Smart.

She nodded. "Give me the gun, and sit down."

Goosebumps rose on my neck – didn't know if I welcomed him there or not.

When the landline phone jangled, Brad raced to answer it. He put his hand over the mouthpiece and gestured to me. "It's Geneva Delbert." He explained to her about the robbery and then gave me the phone.

"Hello, Mrs. Delbert," I said, trying to sound cheerful.

"Are my animals safe?" she asked.

"Dogs are fine. Haven't had a chance to check the rest."

"We can be home by nine tomorrow morning. Let me talk to the police. You, go check my birds, immediately!"

Officer Smart talked to Geneva, then told me, "Miss Garrison, you can't go home until tomorrow. It will be all right for Mr. Franklin to spend the night. The owner vouched for him."

After she consulted Brad, she looked at me. "He will call us when the owners are here. We'll talk to them before we release you."

As the room emptied, a boy delivered a super-sized pizza. Brad gave him a twenty-dollar bill, then set the box in front of me, "Do you eat pepperoni?"

"Anything but anchovies."

He flashed a contagious grin. "Me too."

I started coffee and removed the brownies from one of the grocery sacks still on the counter. The scent of pizza and chocolate permeated the room. Though part of my body hurt, my stomach growled at the pleasant combination.

"Glad Thurber and Thor didn't eat the brownies," I said. "Chocolate makes dogs sick, and we wouldn't have dessert."

Brad plopped four pieces of pizza onto my plate. "Why didn't you tell me you were a pet sitter?"

"I don't know you. Besides, here it's a full-time job."

"That's true. Have you been a pet sitter all your life?"

"No, retired from a more dangerous occupation, teaching kindergarten. And you?" I didn't want to talk but planned to learn why he had a key to that house.

"I'd been a travel agent for several years. When my wife got cancer, I quit work to care for her. I'm advertising guided tours again and plan to have four or five a year. Since I live next door, John gave me a key in case of an emergency – fire, flood, or the rescue of a cute pet sitter. What else do you do?"

Although tired and hurting, I answered, hoping he'd shut up soon. "Volunteer at a nursing home, eat lunch with the girls, play bridge, pet my cat, travel with a friend. Used to square dance but gave that up."

"I'm a bridge player, square dance, hate anchovies, and, of course, travel. We have gobs in common. Let's plan a vacation together."

What? Was he serious? I switched the subject. "What's your favorite bridge convention?"

"Stayman or maybe Blackwood. Fun to have enough points to try a slam."

The conversation changed to memorable games and bidding conventions until I had enough talk to last me the rest of the month.

"Thanks for the pizza," I said. "It's late – have to tend to the birds."

"I'll come too," he offered.

When we entered the sunroom, I gasped. "Some are missing."

"Which ones?"

"The macaw and the African grays. Two cages are gone." I choked, trying to hold my tears inside. "They'll...Geneva will be furious."

Darn. I hadn't purchased insurance, but I couldn't be held responsible for the robbery, could I?

CHAPTER FIFTEEN
THE LIE

Brad stepped in front of me, took hold of my shoulders, and looked into my eyes. "Listen. This isn't your fault. What could you do duct-taped to a chair? When we're done with chores, I'll inform the police the birds are gone. Why would someone steal them?"

I didn't know, though it occurred to me they were valuable. The rest of the animals in the sunroom seemed fine. I scooped cat litter and refreshed the food bowls while Brad went to get carrots from the fridge for Batman.

When I called the goat, he raced toward us, nuzzling our arms for treats. He munched on carrots, then ate the grain I poured into his food bucket.

"That's all for now," I told Brad. "Thanks. I'm going to bed. See you in the morning."

"Are you okay? You had a horrific experience."

"I'm alive. That's a plus."

"Certainly is. May I fix you breakfast in the morning? I'm a pretty versatile chef. Bet you're an excellent cook."

"I do the basics – meatloaf, chili, tuna-noodle casserole, and topnotch ice cubes."

He laughed. "Wake me if you can't sleep. We can have breakfast before John and Geneva get here."

I sped into the guest bedroom and locked the door. On the first page of a notebook, I wrote my robbery story. On the second page, I printed a description of the minister and attempted a sketch. When I got home, maybe I'd send all the information to Officer Smart. She'd be angry, but I had to lie. That tall ogre was more terrifying than the police.

At five-thirty in the morning, I peeked around the corner into the kitchen. Brad sat on a stool reading a newspaper. When he saw me, he said, "We have eggs, bacon, and I'll stir up a batch of pancakes."

"Thanks. I'm starved. Whatever you fix, I'll eat."

I dressed in a worn purple top and jeans. No reason to get spruced up for a man I'd never see again, but before I took the dogs out, I did comb my hair and applied lipstick.

Soon mugs of coffee and plates of scrambled eggs, bacon, and pancakes set on the table. We were both quiet until Brad asked, "When can I come visit you? I doubt you'll be here again."

I didn't answer his question, and he didn't repeat it. That morning he looked fantastic in a gorgeous mint-green short-sleeved shirt. Wonder if he could dance – he'd make an impressive square dance or two-step partner.

He opened his billfold and gave me a business card. "Here's my phone numbers and e-mail address. I haven't been to southwest Missouri in over six months. I can come later this month. We can have supper and go to a Branson show."

"I'll think about it." *Did you forget how to say no?*

Brad nodded. "Promise you'll call when you get home." He paused to study me. "You're a pretty lady, but your hair would improve if you'd let it grow and add a permanent."

My insides swirled. How dare he! "What? Can't believe you said that. I'm not at my best. I had a traumatic day, and you're criticizing my hair!"

He resembled a beat puppy. "Sorry. Only a suggestion. Didn't mean to offend you."

I glared at him but made no promises. Swiping away tears, I raced from the room to pack my suitcase and backpack. Then it was back to the living room to wait until time to leave.

The Gobs of Pets Caper

Startled, I jumped when Geneva burst through the door and raced to the sunroom. When I heard her scream, I sunk lower into the chair, my body trembling. She rushed back, a monstrous scowl on her face. Her hair stood on end, and, for a moment, I thought flames might explode from her head. What an outburst!

"They stole Percy and the grays! Why didn't you tell me? I hate you! Those are expensive birds."

"I'm...I'm sorry. We reported it to the police."

Geneva's fury increased. She waved her arms, yelling and cursing. "Sorry is not enough. You'd better pay for them!"

I backed against a wall, shaking, afraid she'd hit me with her tightened fists. As she charged closer, Brad squeezed between us to block the crazed woman.

In a calm voice, he said, "Quit ranting. I'll vouch for Cookie. She was taped to a chair. No way is she responsible for your loss. If John hadn't disconnected your security system, you'd still have your precious birds."

Geneva wagged her finger at him. "Shut up. It's none of your business."

Officer Smart and another officer came to lead the out-of-control woman to another room. My body stiffened as husband John approached, but he didn't seem angry. He apologized for his wife, then whispered to ask if I could identify the burglar. There was an uneasiness in the way he inquired, but he couldn't be part of the break-in, could he? Before leaving, he deposited a stack of folded bills in my palm. I slid the wad into my pocket without glancing at them. The responsible thing to do was to describe the culprit, but was that safe? Who could I trust? Who should I fear? What if I endangered my friends or Sparky?

Soon Detective Smart arrived. She told John Delbert, "Our team canvassed the area. No one saw anything suspicious except an unusual delivery truck. What is gone besides the birds?"

"I'm making an inventory. We're missing furniture and art – haven't checked the jewelry yet. Some of it is extremely valuable."

The officer motioned for me to join her. My fast heartbeat caused my ears to throb. I pressed my elbows into my sides to stop the beating.

"Good morning, Miss Garrison. Have you thought of anything else?"

"No. I haven't."

"Let's hear your version again."

I fisted my hands to keep from trembling. "I already told you."

"Repeating it may give us more details."

She tapped a pen against the chair and waited. Her eyebrows scrunched together, and her lower lip stuck out, similar to a parent who learned it was advisable for their child to repeat kindergarten. I told my memorized lie, gritting my teeth and pausing often. I didn't want to say too much. When done, I asked, "Is that all? I want to go home."

Officer Smart sighed and frowned. Another officer gave me a business card. "Contact us when your memory works better. Drive carefully. Chloroform might make you groggy."

As we ignored Geneva's glowering looks, Brad escorted me out the front to my Buick.

"Thanks for defending me," I said.

"No problem. Call me when you get home."

I ducked when he reached for a hug. Instead, he grinned and squeezed my shoulders. I locked the car doors and clutched the steering wheel. As I drove away, his face appeared in the rear-view mirror, waving until my car was out of sight.

It felt as if the ordeal lasted days, but it was over. Time to have a calmer life.

Wrong again!

CHAPTER SIXTEEN

HOME AT LAST

After three stops and too much coffee, I arrived home. Sparky greeted me with a loud yowl. I dropped my suitcase and fell into the living room recliner. He jumped onto my lap and meowed several times, then purred.

The answering machine blinked four times. Figured it was probably pet sitting inquiries. I called Polly before listening to the messages.

"I'm home," I said. "Thanks for checking on Sparky."

"I've been worried. Why are you back so soon? What happened?"

"Did Sparky behave?"

"Of course, he's always a gentleman. Why are you home?"

Considering Polly's psychic tendencies, I was not eager to tell her about my experience in St. Louis. "Uh, the family had an emergency. How are you?"

"Albert ignores me, but he hasn't left. Will I see you at lunch bunch?"

"Not this week. Can you come for brunch tomorrow? I have a new poppy seed recipe, and I'll explain about the trip."

"Okay, but why not tell me now?" She paused, but when I didn't respond, said, "Never mind. See you at ten."

The first calls on my answering machine were from potential clients, and the third, Eunice Taylor. Then I heard my daughter, Marsha. "Where are you? You're not answering e-mails or calls. Wish you'd buy that cell phone. Would mid-June work for the girls to come? Please call me."

What could I do? I had to avoid the minister, forget Brad, and make pet sitting plans. My life had changed from boring to confusing to frightening. What a mess!

I agreed to talk to a cat owner in the building but refused a pit bull job. Not opposed to any breed, but the woman's bragging about her fierce dog made it a no-brainer. Also, I shouldn't stray too far from home in case the sinister minister located me.

Before I phoned my daughter, she called. "Is something wrong?" she asked.

"No, I took a short trip. I did buy a cell phone. Ready for the number?"

After I recited it, she questioned me more.

"Where'd you go?" she asked.

"St. Louis. I'll let you know later when the girls can come."

In order to avoid the subjects of pet sitting and St. Louis, I asked about her classroom. She chattered for fifteen minutes about teaching struggles. After that, the subject changed to my grandchildren's school activities and Eli's oppositional behavior. That last topic bothered me, but I tried not to ever comment about anything she told me.

Next, I called Eunice Taylor. "This is Cookie. How are you and Og?"

"We're good. Can you come down, dear? We need to talk."

"Be right there," I said, hoping it wasn't about Geneva's robbery.

In Eunice's apartment, I parked myself in a comfy overstuffed chair. Og jumped into my lap for a scratch while my aged friend prepared tea. She waved her hand at the dog, and he leapt off, sitting at attention while his owner poured the light green liquid into delicate mint-colored cups, then carried a tray of baked goods to a coffee table.

"Have a homemade treat with your tea," she invited.

The Gobs of Pets Caper

I selected an appetizing cookie with frosting on the top. Yum. It was soft with a melt-in-your-mouth pumpkin flavor. "Wow! These are great," I said. Before I could continue, she interrupted me.

"I'm so sorry for your difficulties at my niece's house. Geneva is too emotional. The bird loss is not your fault. My goodness, she said the burglar taped you to a chair. Let me pay for your trouble. I'm responsible for what happened because I recommended you."

"Oh, no, Mr. Delbert might not have told Geneva, but he gave me, uh, plenty of money." I didn't mention it was a roll of four one-hundred-dollar bills.

"Surprised he did that. He's usually a stingy jerk. Let me know if either of them bothers you again. Geneva is nice to me because she expects me to will all my assets to her. I doubt I'll do that, and I don't plan to die soon."

After playing fetch with Og, I went to Larry and Barb Hernandez's apartment on the second floor. I agreed to care for their one-year-old orange tabby for four days. Within thirty minutes, I'm home, comfortably stretched out on the sofa with Sparky purring on my chest.

"I'm watching a cat named Daisy."

He jumps down. "Yowl, yowl."

"Hush! She's a friendly girl."

"Meow-ow-ow."

At nine-thirty that evening, I climbed my tired body into bed. My eyes stayed closed until the landline phone rang the next morning at seven o'clock.

"It's Brad. Did I wake you?"

"Yes. How did you find my number?"

"Not challenging. You're in the phone book, kid. Tomorrow I've a meeting in Branson. There's a square dance at Northview tonight. Do you have an outfit?"

"Yes, two dresses, but I haven't worn them in ages — thought they don't do costumes anymore."

"This is a charity event, a special dress-up dance. You'd be doing me a favor. I need a partner.

"Not me. There are always extra gals."

"I'd rather dance with you."

This guy didn't give up. I hesitated, my lips forming the word "no," but thought what fun it would be to square dance again. "Okay. Call me when you're close. I'll zip over to Northview."

"But I can pick you up," he said.

I heard his disappointment but ignored it. "I'll meet you there, or I won't go."

You'll regret this. Mom, what harm could there be in a square dance?

I carried a step ladder into the bedroom closet to reach a plastic bag from the top shelf. When I emptied the contents, a fluffy slip, petti pants, and two dresses tumbled onto the bed.

I slipped the red, white, and blue one over my head. It was for a demonstration dance group with the married Jeremy. The other was a black and yellow one with a full skirt with rows of ruffles. It fit better but wasn't as sexy.

The phone interrupted my decision. "Glad I caught you," said Polly. "Sorry, but I'm canceling lunch. Albert has a doctor's appointment. He's got cancer. Prostate, but people survive that. Isn't that better than another woman?"

"Cancer can kill. Why was he so secretive?"

"Oh, he anticipated the worst. Thought he'd die or end up in a nursing home. Said he didn't want to burden me. Isn't that loveable?"

Sounded stupid to me.

"What happened in St. Louis?" asked Polly.

"Nothing important. Let me know what the doctors say."

I needed to talk to someone, but not Polly. Olivia was a better choice. After several rings, she answered my call.

"Where are you?" she asked.

"Home. How about brunch on Wednesday at my place? I'd like your opinion about something."

"Works for me. Can't wait for an update on your trip. I'll bring fall vacation ideas."

If you keep running around, you will be dead by fall. Shut up, Mom.

Maybe there was reason to worry. Why did I agree to go square dancing? That was a foolish choice. I had better quit pet sitting and stay home with Sparky until the bad guys were caught. Perhaps the location of anyone could be traced.

In spite of that revelation, I didn't think that included me.

Wrong again!

CHAPTER SEVENTEEN

SQUARE DANCE FUN

On Tuesday, Sparky watched me dress in a billowing slip and position the black and yellow ruffled dress over it. In the bathroom, I removed lipstick, liquid make-up, rouge, and a curling iron from a drawer.

Brad's call interrupted my preparations. "I'm at the Strafford exit. What's your address?"

Might be safer if I rode with him. No, I'd be okay. "I'm driving my own car. You told me the dance is at seven o'clock. You're early."

"I thought we'd eat first, or you can cook."

"No cooking." What should I say? What should I do?

He broke the silence. "Have you been to Cracker Barrel? It's not fancy but has predictable food."

"Sure. Meet you there around five-thirty."

"Hey, purrball. Guess it's dinner out tonight." I was irritated and thrilled at the same time. I'd tolerate the dinner to go to a square dance, especially a dress-up one.

When I pulled into the restaurant lot, I noticed Brad on the front porch in one of the rockers. He walked toward my car as I pulled into a spot beside his BMW.

We both ordered the daily special – turkey with mashed potatoes, dressing, and green beans. While we waited on our food, Brad explained what we'd do on his upcoming bus tour to Chicago.

I interrupted his chatter. "Stop. I'm not going anywhere with you."

"You can have a discounted rate."

I tipped my head up and stared at the ceiling, trying to think how to respond. "One square dance doesn't mean anything else – certainly not taking a trip with you!"

"Okay. By the way, kid, you're a knock-out in that outfit."

"Without a perm in my hair?" Though I intended it a joke, my words dripped with sarcasm.

"Sorry. That was rude. Please forget it."

"I'll try. I am thrilled to go square dancing but might mess up – haven't been in years."

"The male has the difficult part. You'll be fine. Just relax and follow me."

His BMW and my Buick turned onto Kearney Street and into the Northview Center lot. At the entrance, I watched the crowd assemble while Brad paid our entry fees. Several people looked familiar. Then one of the members of the demonstration team recognized me.

She waved and joined us. "Hi, Cookie. It's been ages. Who's this fetching fellow?" She extended her hand to Brad. "I'm Kate Landers."

Brad shook it, said his name, and then complimented Kate's attire. Charisma oozed from him as he looked at her with his searing blue eyes. She giggled, straightened her back, and stuck out her chest. I stifled a laugh.

A booming sound system announcement interrupted the encounter. "Square up. It's seven o'clock."

We trailed Kate to a square with her partner and two other couples. The eight of us exchanged hugs and introduced ourselves. It had been years since I had square danced. What if I embarrassed myself?

Over blaring music, the caller announced, "Ladies, step forward and wave to your partner. Now let's all do-si-do. Swing your partner." Brad whirled me around, lifting his arm for me to twirl under it.

Our caller, Cowboy Bob, was dressed in western attire with an oversized hat, a purple western shirt, and lavish matching boots. "Grand turnout tonight. Welcome. Let's practice some basic calls." He retaught several steps, then sang "Bill Bailey Won't You Please Come Home" for an easy first set. All eight in our square laughed and smiled at our success.

Brad and I danced all the tips and three of the line dances. During the intermission, the dancers ambled toward the food tables, where sweets, fruit, and mini-sandwiches awaited us. An attractive blond gal stared at us from across the room, then came nearer.

She waved and smiled. "It is you, Brad. What are you doing out of St. Louis?"

He gestured at me. "Cookie Garrison, meet Margo – a friend of mine."

When she glared at me for longer than appropriate, I studied the ceiling. She started to say something, but Brad interrupted her.

"Margo, how wonderful to see you again. It's been ages. To answer your question, I have business down south, thought I'd catch a dance on the way." He pointed across the room. "Is that your partner in the food line? He looks familiar."

"Yes, it's Tom. Better go. He tends to be anxious when he loses me."

Brad loaded two plates with sandwiches and cheesecake while I watched Margo, hoping to learn what she didn't say. After the food break, the dancing progressed to more difficult calls, but I managed each tip with no significant errors. Before I realized it, the time had come for the dancers to join hands in a huge circle. We did a grand right and left to thank the caller and end the night's fun. I excused myself when I noticed Margo hastening across the dance floor toward the bathroom. She stood at the mirror, combing her hair.

"Hi, Margo. This was a fun dance."

"They all are. You have a gorgeous man. Been dating long?"

"We're not a couple. Recently, I met him in St. Louis. Tonight, he needed a partner."

"Really? You're the image of his wife. Are you related to her?"

A pang hit my chest, but I tried to not show any distress. "No. I haven't met his family. I've heard we all have a twin someplace." I wanted to ask about the wife, but the words stuck in my throat.

Margo frowned, then moved toward the exit. She turned to study me again. "Do you believe he'd have any difficulty finding a partner? Brad's an interesting fellow, draws single gals like flies to a cow pie. Don't get too attached to him. You'll regret it."

I had assumed Brad was a widower. Did other dancers notice a similarity to the wife? I squinted to hold back my tears with no luck, though splashing cold water on my face helped.

The door swung open, and Kate entered. "You look pale. Are you sick?"

"Uh, no, got a little over-heated." *You're lying again.*

"Your partner's a doll – better than that Jeremy you dated. Any chance you'd give me Brad's phone number?"

I told her no, resisting a rude comment, then waited five minutes before going back on the dance floor.

"Are you okay?" asked Brad. "Kate said you don't feel well."

"Had a slight wave of nausea."

"Are you pregnant?" he joked.

I made myself laugh. "That'd make the Guinness book of records. Thanks for supper and the dance. Forgot how fun square dances are."

"Me too. You were a great partner – didn't miss a call."

As we walked toward the exit, Brad waved at all the dancers. When we reached the Buick, he blocked the car door with his arm. "May I call you?"

"I..., I'd..., not now." *Why can't you say no?* He's so persuasive, Mom.

"You look sad," observed Brad. "What will turn your frown upside down?"

"It's been a tough week. Move your arm, please."

When he did, I attempted to force a cheery expression, though I had no happy feelings.

As I drove away, I looked in the rearview mirror to see if he was still there. Instead, I saw a red delivery truck, identical to the one in front of Geneva's house in St. Louis. Too frightened to find out if there was a dent in the side, I yearned to get home. When I managed to stop shaking, I thought about the square dance. The dance itself was fantastic. I'd never had a partner as capable and attractive as Brad. However, I failed to stop thinking about his wife and the earlier hair suggestion. The wife must have, or had, long hair and a perm. Did he want me to look like her? Was she still alive?

At the apartment, I slowed into the front parking lot, then noticed another red truck a block behind me. Gripping the steering wheel, I raced to the back lot. Trucks were tailing me.

Could that be the same one I'd seen three times? Could the sinister minister or his partner be the driver?

CHAPTER EIGHTEEN

HELP FOR COOKIE

I sped behind the building and waited as the red truck barreled around the corner of the building. The vehicle was definitely the one from St. Louis, but I couldn't identify the driver. The truck had a dent and chipped paint on the passenger side. I laid down on the front seat of the car and waited for fifteen minutes, body shaking the entire time. When I sat up, the lot was empty, except for the bull terrier pulling Ben. I dashed out of the Buick and ran into the building, skipping every other step up the stairs to my apartment.

I unlocked and bolted the door, not answering the landline phone when it rang. My fear increased as the answering machine recorded another warning. Shuddering, I visualized the sinister minister.

"Yes, we are watching you. You are a wise lady not to give information to anyone. Your friends, Polly? Olivia? Are they ever at your apartment? Keep your mouth shut, and nothing tragic will happen to your family, friends, or cat, Cas-san-dra."

He knew where I lived. Polly? Olivia? Sparky? Somebody must have tapped my phone. How dare he terrorize me more! Rage mixed with fear of what this wicked man could do made me shudder. On wobbly legs, I double-checked the deadbolt on my entry and closed all the blinds. I picked up Sparky and hurried to my bedroom to dial Brad on my cell. The phone rang and rang until he answered.

I asked, "Can you join me mid-way for lunch on Thursday?"

"What? Cookie? I can't understand you. You're talking too fast. You sound strange."

After swallowing several times, I repeated the question at a slower pace. We agreed on a time to meet at a family restaurant he suggested. Olivia and then Brad — one or both of them might have a reasonable idea about what to do next. I reclined on the bed beside Sparky imagining my body as a melting blob, relaxing until my panic left. Calmer, I fixed a sandwich then checked my e-mail. I needed to reply to Marsha's last one and had a new message from gobs of pets. Geneva must have offered me an apology for her rudeness, but that wasn't the case.

Her e-mail said:

> You will contact your pet insurance company for the cost of my birds. The total is $6,500. When can I expect a check?

I copied the message. No way would or could I pay for those birds!

Before Olivia arrived on Wednesday, I slid a breakfast casserole into the oven and arranged a fruit bowl. Since she was allergic to cats, Sparky stayed in the bedroom. When the doorbell rang, I caught a glimpse of my friend through the security peephole. I jerked open the door, pulled her inside, and threw the deadbolt.

"Whoa. What's the matter?" asked Olivia.

"Someone's after me."

"Have you lost your senses? No one is after you."

"Food will be ready in ten minutes, then I'll tell you about the robbery during my St. Louis stay." I poured steaming coffee into mugs, but my hands shook, forcing me to spill most of it.

"Calm down," Olivia said. "Let me do that. Scary, but intriguing. Perhaps it will be a juicy episode for my next book."

Olivia teased her friends, often telling us we were in her mystery novels. In her last book, one of her scenes did seem familiar.

"I have a dilemma," I said. "But promise you won't replay it in your books."

"Can't do that, but you're welcome to approve my work before it's published."

I pondered her answer before the St. Louis story poured out of my mouth.

"Wow," exclaimed Olivia. "Robbery, threats, mysterious man. How can I not use such juicy drama? What will you do next?"

"Try to control my fear and not do something dangerous. Any advice?"

"Fax or call the police department in St. Louis. You're breaking the law by withholding information. Besides, you don't lie. Only members of Congress do that." She wrinkled her nose before she smiled.

"I'm afraid – more scared than when we were lost in Chicago, more scared than the fire on the cruise ship, more scared than ever in my entire life. Maybe I'll buy a gun."

"Don't take this the wrong way, but you're clumsy. Have you ever owned one? You know the bad guys won't disappear."

"Okay, no guns. Let's change the subject. Did you bring fall vacation information?"

Olivia dragged stacks of travel stuff from her bag. "Here are brochures on cruises and guided tours, or we can drive west on a road trip. Let's make a list of possibilities."

She had lists for everything. We waded through pamphlets and brochures while she wrote down trip information. By noon, I'd had enough. "Thanks, but I'm not in the mood to do more."

"Okay. I'll leave the info for you." We both glanced down the hall. Seeing no one, she hurried away. I watched out the window as she drove off in her Toyota Scion.

After double-checking the locks and blinds, I let Sparky out of the bedroom. He meowed to go onto the deck until he tired of nagging. I tried to read my Evanovich novel but couldn't clear my mind to stick with it. Sparky leapt onto the phone table. Two minutes later, it rang, and the answering machine clicked on, but no one left a message.

The next morning, I rolled out of bed at five, wide awake. After removing three outfits from the closet, I chose a maroon top with dark slacks. I spent more time than usual on hair and make-up, adding a pair of dangling earrings. In the cabinet above the commode, removing a collection of perfume containers. I noticed a bottle of Charlie, a long-ago gift from Carl. "You won't care if I use this, will you?" No one answered as I sprayed it on my arms.

Before leaving, I looked both ways into the hall, relieved it was empty. I scurried down the stairs to the building exit, ran to the car, and sped onto Battlefield Street, not able to relax until I pulled onto I-44.

I had departed early to have plenty of time to arrive at Pop's Eatery. Parking near the front door, I took a mini-nap until a tapping erupted on the car window. Ouch! My head hit the car roof. Brad gazed through the window with a puzzled expression. I rolled it down.

"Sorry to startle you," he said. "Did you have a difficult drive?

"No. Just haven't been sleeping well."

As we walked toward the restaurant door, I wondered if anyone besides me thought he resembled the actor. That day, my Brad wore a luxurious shirt the color of Granny Smith apples, with tantalizing tan slacks that fit him perfectly. He must pay big bucks for his clothes.

When he situated his arm around my waist, I quivered. Did I come for his advice or just to see him again? *Why do you bother with this man?* Mom married Dad when they were teenagers. After he died, she had no interest in another male for her remaining twenty years.

After Carl died, she disapproved of my involvement with anyone else.

"You smell wonderful," said Brad.

My insides smiled, appreciating the compliment. When we entered the eatery, a hostess bustled over to seat us. "I'm Cindy. Smoking or none?"

"None," I said. "Please show us a table in a private area."

She led us to a small room and gave us each a menu. "The place is yours unless we get busy. Be here in five with water."

After she left, Brad broke the silence. "How's pet sitting?"

"Okay. If I'm distant, don't take it personally."

"Let's talk, then we'll go dancing later."

"No dancing. I need help. Hope I can trust you."

He didn't speak for a few moments, then said, "Let's order, then I'll tell you all about my life."

The menu included six home-cooked specials. We both ordered the pot roast. Before it came, Brad began his life story, relating the pleasures of growing up with his four siblings on a farm close to Joplin. He then shared stories of college life, falling in love, and marrying when he was twenty-one, but he didn't say anything about his wife's illness. I learned he had become an engineer, and, after retirement, a travel agent. He beamed when he showed me pictures of his two sons and three grandchildren. Last, he told me about the painful death of his wife of forty years. Nothing he mentioned indicated an inkling of deception. I believed it all.

Waitress Cindy brought two heaping plates of beef, mashed potatoes, and broccoli. "Be back with the rolls. Do you want catsup, Tabasco, or Tallulah?"

"What? Oh, bring them all," said Brad, adding to me, "Maybe she meant Chalupa."

"Or Bankhead?"

He winked at me as we watched the waitress line up bottles of catsup, Tabasco, and Chalupa hot sauce on the table. When she brought a basket of steaming rolls, I couldn't resist adorning one with strawberry jelly. Yum! I loved fresh bread.

Brad chuckled at my eagerness. "Your husband passed away. Was he ill long?"

I bit my lower lip, then spit out an explanation. "He didn't die from natural causes. A drunk driver swerved into his lane, totaled his Jeep, and killed him instantly." My words brought back bad images. I excused myself to go to the restroom, hoping to hold back the tears.

Ten minutes later, back at our table, Brad pulled out my chair. He kissed the top of my head. "Loss is harsh. He'd want you to get on with a happy life."

Not willing to talk about anything but my current situation, I said, "I'm scared. First, here's an e-mail from Geneva. Can she sue me?"

He slammed his fist on the table. "Damn the woman. She can try anything, but she won't win. John had the security system disconnected and didn't have insurance on those stupid birds. Not your problem." He tore the paper into bits and threw them into the air. "Gone. What else?"

I took two deep breaths, hesitant to admit the next one. "This is worse. I lied to Officer Smart. That was a mistake. Here is what really happened." I gave Brad an envelope with a summary of the stay at the Delbert's house and a sketch of the robber.

"Of course, you'll inform the police. You may need to go back to St. Louis." He noticed the address on the envelope. "Were you planning to mail this to Officer Smart?"

"I'd rather you give it to her," I said.

"Won't do that. She could assume I knew the truth but didn't tell."

"Sorry. That didn't occur to me. The minister has found me. I'm getting threatening phone calls, and I'm being followed."

Our waitress came back with more menus. "How about supper? We have some great evening specials, or check out our desserts." She pointed to a blackboard with six tasty possibilities written in white chalk.

"Let's end with apple pie ala mode," said Brad. "Then we need to finish a talk. Guess we can pay you rent."

Cindy giggled. "No rent. Stay as long as you like, but I'd appreciate a tip."

We relished warm pie, topped with scoops of melting ice cream. I savored each bite of the crisp apples, cinnamon, and flaky crust. The dessert soothed my frustrations.

"A question for you," said Brad. "If you're so scared, how come you risked driving here?"

I traced my fingers over the cracks in the wood table.

"Cookie, look at me. Did you want to see me again?"

"Perhaps. I'm confused, scared, angry, not myself. I like you, but you're so, so pushy and..."

He smiled, then ate his last bite of pie. "Sorry. Thanks for telling me. I'll do better. Here's a plan. There's a mailbox out front where you can drop the envelope. Second, you can take my revolver for protection. Third, let's switch cars for a while. The guy won't expect you to drive mine."

"Cars, okay, but I never handled a gun. I might shoot my toe off – don't like to bleed.

"We can do the car trade today. Now, May I have your address?"

I wrote it on a napkin. "Here. You'd better be a nice guy, or I'll learn to shoot a gun and practice on you."

"I'm a great guy. Also, let me know if you get arrested for withholding information. I have an excellent lawyer."

"Are you serious?"

"Probably won't happen, but it's good to be prepared."

"What had I done? What would Sparky do if I went to jail?"

When we reached the black BMW, the whiff and feel of the rich leather upholstery poured through my body. I scooted into the driver's seat, knowing I'd be safe in this fabulous car. Brad leaned forward and kissed me on the cheek.

"Cookie Garrison, a car is replaceable, but you're not. Don't drive too fast, and be watchful. I'll call you on your cell tonight."

All the way home, I listened to the rhythm of the tires striking the payment. When they hit rough patches on the road, I imagined they told me to "take it slow, take it slow." At home, the back parking lot was empty except for Eunice walking Og and people unloading a U-

Haul – no red trucks or mean-looking men. Maybe I'd been imagining trouble that wasn't there.

I soon found out it wasn't my imagination. More scary times awaited me.

CHAPTER NINETEEN
DOWN THE TRASH CHUTE

After the U-Haul left, I raced to the nearest entry, burst up the stairs, and flew into my apartment, nearly falling over Sparky. I grabbed the edge of the counter to steady myself as the cat attempted to wrap his body around my legs. I picked him up and accepted a feline hug. "

After I change clothes, I'll go see Daisy cat, but I'll be back soon. It's unsafe for me to wander these halls."

"Meow. Meow."

I avoided the blinking answering machine, afraid it might be another call from the minister. Heading out the door, the cell in my pocket vibrated.

"Are you home now?" asked Brad.

"Yes. Didn't see anyone. After one cat visit, it's bedtime. Thanks for the car."

"Wasn't enthused about your Buick, but it got me home. How about stopping your pet sitting for a while?"

"Just one cat in the building. I'll be careful."

"I may not allow you to keep my car unless you agree to go square dancing with me again."

"Hmm. Are you blackmailing me?"

"No, I didn't mean it that way."

"You tell me not to pet sit, but you want me to go dancing. Really?"

"You're safe with me. I have a gun and won't shoot off my toe. I do need my car soon. I have another out-of-town trip in a couple of weeks."

"If you insist," I said, smiling as his captivating chuckle traveled across the miles. Not wise to encourage him, but I hoped he could be a faithful friend. However, I sensed that might not be enough for him. Why didn't such a handsome guy have a girlfriend? What if he had cancer or some other grave disease and died? Goosebumps traveled down my spine at those thoughts. As I massaged my temples, I peered into the hall. No one was there.

I hastened to the cat's apartment. A mat announced *Attack Cat Lives Here.* Inside, Daisy watched while I refreshed her water, food bowls, then scooped clumps of litter into a paper bag. When I collapsed into a chair, the tabby landed in my lap with a thump.

"Whoa, girl." She purred as I stroked her soft fur. "You're a sweetie. Your owner ought to discard that mat. You won't attack anything."

On the way to the elevator, I saw one person, a young girl on a power walk. In my apartment, I bolted the door, glad to be safe at home, glad I lived in a locked building, glad I had Sparky to calm me. Perhaps we would watch Johnny Carson reruns. Instead, I decided to sleep. When I nestled under my thick down comforter, Sparky curled beside me. I embraced him, soothed by his soft purrs but wondered about the phone messages.

After thirty minutes, I moved my cat and went into the living room, prepared to advance the machine if I heard the minister. Instead, the first message was from Manhunter Marge, gushing about how she missed my stories and insisting we go to a dance at the Elks Club.

Next one was from my daughter. "I read your last e-mail. Are you okay? Why can't the girls visit this summer?"

I picked up the cell and called her. "I didn't say the girls couldn't visit. Just can't set a date yet. There are a few things to do first."

"Are you doing something weird?"

"No, just a new project. I'm tired. I'll call you soon."

The third call was from Nora. "Hi. We missed you at lunch bunch? I'll stop by your place tomorrow."

Yuck! No way would I answer if I saw that dingbat through my security peephole.

Then the fourth message began. "Ca-sand-ra. Good, you're remembering not to...."

Heart thumping and palms perspiring, I disconnected the machine. In my bedroom, I locked the door and plastered my body against the wall, sweat dripping off my forehead. In a while, the panic subsided, but a strange dream awoke me at one o'clock. In my dream, I was chased by a giant man. To block out the vision of the pursuit, I turned on the radio. A KWTO talk show host discussed government cover-ups of alien abductions as I dozed back to sleep. Soon my eyes were wide open again, running from hundreds of men in space suits leading pit bulls. The red numerals on the bedside clock said 4:00. An hour later, I slept again until the doorbell chimed at eight o'clock.

I tiptoed to the security peephole to stare into the hallway. A short man dressed in a navy suit wore a red necktie and held a briefcase. Must be a salesman, but no way I'd risk opening my door to anyone. My body froze when a rattling meant he'd tried to open the door. Dread knotted my stomach. After the clock ticked ten times, I checked the hall again – no one there, but, within minutes, the doorbell rang again. When I didn't answer, there was a knock, and I heard Nora Alexander say my name. I tiptoed to the peephole to make sure it was her. Adrenaline surged through me as the navy-suited man's arms stretched around Nora's body. The minister joined the short fellow, and together they jammed a rag over her mouth and pulled her away.

I dialed 9-1-1. "Men attacked a woman! They're dragging her down the hall."

The dispatcher requested more information which I gave her, but I must have been babbling.

She yelled, "Calm down. Speak slower. Don't hang up. Help will be there soon."

I cracked open the door to get a better view of the hallway, flinching as the minister and his assistant stopped in front of the trash chute. I gasped as I watched them thrust Nora's legs into the receptacle. Her body jerked as if she'd had a seizure. The minister took hold of her shoulders and shoved with both his hands. I heard her scream weaken as she traveled down the chute.

All of a sudden, Sparky flew between my feet and stormed down the hall, faster than a flying Frisbee. His loud hissing became a low growl, and the hair raised on his arched back. Amazed, I wanted to cheer him on.

"Are you there?" asked the 9-1-1 operator.

"Sparky. Come here." I trembled with fear, but he ignored my pleas. He snarled, flew through the air, and landed on the man with the red tie. The accomplice flailed his arms, but my boy held on tight as his claws dug into the assailant's head. What a cat!

"Damn it, get him off! He's scratching my face! I'm bleeding. Kill him!"

In one quick motion, the minister snatched Sparky and forced him into the chute. Chaos followed. Obscenities floated down the hall. Blood stained the hall carpet. People opened their doors to observe the commotion. The phone operator pleaded for an answer.

"They put Nora and my cat down the trash chute!" I yelled into the cell.

"Did you say a trash chute? It's illegal to make prank calls."

"It's a large chute. Will you please send the police?"

"Police and ambulance are on the way. Are you okay?"

"Of course not. I'm contacting more help." My emergency numbers were posted on the fridge. First, I called the office manager and then the building's security firm. Loud banging interrupted my efforts at reaching anyone else.

"Police. Anyone in there?"

Darn! I opened the door to Officers Bob Hope and Tom Jones. Were they the only policemen in Springfield?

"Ah-ha, it's the pet sitter," said Officer Hope. "Maybe time to issue a citation for too many calls."

"Hey, mister. Nora and Sparky were pushed down the trash chute. Show some compassion!"

He hooted, "You're kidding, right?"

Officer Jones said, "I don't think she is."

The manager and two men wearing security uniforms rushed toward us. The six of us hurried to the elevator. When the door slid open, Brad stood there with a bunch of artificial roses. Why hadn't he called first? Was this a harbinger of future interruptions? Then I recalled, I had his BMW.

He gave me the flowers and said, "Brought you these. Thought the cat might eat real ones."

"What are you doing?"

"Nora and Sparky are in trouble. We're on our way to the basement to rescue them."

"Why are they there?"

"The minister and his buddy pushed them down the trash chute."

"Must be a big chute."

Funny, but I couldn't laugh. Instead, I provided Brad an explanation as the elevator ground to a halt.

The manager used a gold-pronged key to admit us to the basement, releasing a potent odor. One of the security guys opened the heavy basement doors. They creaked to admit crisp, cool air into the cavernous room. The manager pointed toward the east end of the building. "Your floor empties into those bins."

Sparky's yowls guided us across the cement floor to the end container. It reeked, a pungent combination of cat litter and spoiled food with a tint of rose fragrance. Sparky leapt out of the bin and flung himself into my arms, coating me with pieces of veggies, paper, and cat litter.

The cat jumped onto my shoulder. "Meow. Meow."

"Yuck, you stink, but I love you anyway."

Nora's shoes protruded from the trash mess. The men removed her and laid her on the floor. I stooped to scrape food and assorted pieces of debris from her hair. Her whole body shook as she clasped my wrist to pull herself up. "I'm never coming here again." She collapsed, banging her head on the cement floor.

Sirens blared as an ambulance screeched inside, and paramedics rushed to the now unconscious Nora. Within ten minutes, they had her loaded onto a gurney and on the way to the hospital.

Officer Hope grunted and stared at me with an expression of disbelief. "Jones, write down the contact info for these security people. Miss Garrison, let's go someplace else? It stinks down here."

"Call me Cookie. I see you more than most of my friends. How about my apartment? I'll make coffee, and I have leftover donuts."

Officer Hope flashed a wide grin. "Good plan."

Sparky cuddled into my arms as we all boarded the elevator to my apartment.

I pointed to the kitchen table. "Have a seat. I'll change clothes."

I washed the basement yuck off my body, locked Sparky in the bathroom, and hurried to dress in my best outfit. Then I dialed Polly to ask if she'd notify Nora's daughter that her mother was in Cox Hospital. Polly knew the family; I didn't.

"What's the matter with her?" asked Polly.

"It's complicated. How was the trip to the doctor?"

"We're optimistic."

"Hurry up!" yelled one of the officers.

"Who's there?" asked Polly.

"Have to go. I'll let you know later."

"Nice outfit," said Officer Hope. "You're a lot of trouble, but you're sure a spunky gal."

Brad touched my arm and whispered, "These fellows are quirky but can help you. Let them hear your story."

I didn't want anyone else involved in the mess I'd made. It would be awkward to admit my lie. Often, the trouble with lies is one causes another. However, it was time to clear up all the confusion I'd created.

"Officers. I have a wild but true tale that will explain why Nora and Sparky were in the trash bin. I hope you can advise me about what to do next."

Officer Hope smiled, so broad most of his teeth showed. He must have considered that a terrific compliment. "Jones, record this."

Officer Jones set up a device while I found napkins, leftover donuts, and coffee mugs. Officer Hope gobbled down a chocolate donut and seized a second one while I explained about my pet sitting experiences at the Delbert's house. He chuckled about my being duct-taped, but his demeanor became serious when I finished my story with the threats the minister had made.

"Now the burglar leaves messages. I didn't listen to the final one."

"Play it now," said Officer Hope.

I nodded, pushed the replay button, and shivered at the minister's clear, enunciated words. "Cas-san-dra, good you're remembering not to report me. I didn't see Olivia yesterday. Did you insist she not come? My friend has a code to your building. You will be cooperative, or we will use it. We know your every move."

"Bold fellow," said the officer. "We'll send the tech crew over here. Your apartment might be bugged. I'll contact the St. Louis police and try to explain why you lied."

"Just thought of something else," I said. "When I was in St. Louis, a red delivery truck drove by Delbert's house. Now red trucks are following me." I dug into my purse for the scrap of paper where I'd written the license number of the last one I saw.

Hope thrust it toward Jones. "Run this in the cruiser."

Ten minutes later, the officers had a name and location of a property. Officer Hope's face erupted with another smile. "Might catch ourselves a crook today. That's the old downtown hotel on Main Street. Owner's name is Charles Wilson. Let's request a search warrant. We can buzz over there – see if anyone's home."

My earlier fear transferred into determination. "Me too. I can identify the birds and some of the furnishings."

"Nope," said Officer Hope. "We can't take a civilian."

"What if we follow you?"

The officer twisted his mouth and bit his upper lip, pausing in thought. "If anyone asks, I didn't give you permission. You know it could be dangerous."

Determined not to let fear overcome me, I said, "I will rescue those birds." I didn't feel brave; it was just something I had to do. I didn't know why – excitement, anger, or revenge. Whatever the reasons, I adored those birds, especially Percy.

Brad whispered to himself as I locked the door, and we hurried to catch up with the policemen. Inside my apartment, Sparky yowled.

"What's his problem?" asked Brad.

"He worries a lot."

"Smart cat. You should pay attention to him."

"I often do. It's okay if you don't go."

"I'll not abandon you, but since it's my car, I'll drive."

Brad parked on the street while the cop car entered the empty parking lot beside the hotel. Immediately, another vehicle arrived with two more policemen. After a short discussion, the four walked to the rear of the building. When I reached for the BMW's handle, Brad grasped my arm. "Wait. Be patient. Let's see what happens."

That day patience was not a virtue I possessed.

CHAPTER TWENTY

THE RESCUE

I jerked away and slammed the passenger door, then jogged toward the rear of the aging structure. The entrance was partially blocked, but I shifted sideways to fit through the narrow opening. Ahead of me, the four officers worked their way through a maze of stacked furniture. Spotting ornate legs, I stooped to examine a dining table and the matching China cabinet.

Brad caught up with me. "Is that Geneva and John's furniture?"

"Yes. See those unusual wood carvings on the legs."

Chirps and shrieks drifted from above. We stopped talking. First, we heard the familiar birthday song, and then one that resembled a human scream.

"Cookie's cool. Cookie's cool."

"That's Geneva's macaw," said Brad. "Impressive! He learned your name."

"I think he likes me. Percy and the African grays must be on the top floor. I'm going to find them."

"That's not safe. Let's hunt the policemen."

I couldn't wait. Percy needed me. Several years before I'd been in this building. It dated back to the 1930s when it was a busy hotel. Much later, it opened as a flea market and then an October funhouse. At the bottom of the ancient stairs, I tried to visualize the layout. There was no elevator, only old narrow steps all the way to a fourth floor.

The items on the second and third floors were more organized than on the first. I waded through hundreds of paintings, then appliances, followed by various tools and machinery. Ascending the steep steps to the fourth level, my knees weakened as if a crowbar had mashed both of them. But I was determined to find Percy.

As I neared the next landing, I yelled, "Percy, where are you?"

"Percy's cool. Cookie's cool."

The screeching increased, and a whiff of wet feathers combined with rancid bird droppings made me sneeze. Exhausted, I rested for a moment, then eased down the hallway where cages lined the back wall. In one, the African grays perched side by side. I spied Percy in a smaller cage at the end of the row. He paced back and forth, cocked his head, and greeted me, "Cookie's cool."

"Glad to see you, too, Percy. Hey, Brad! Found the birds. Where are you?" I yelled his way.

Behind me, I heard, "Too bad for you and your boyfriend. You can't seem to avoid trouble, Cas-san-dra."

A knot the size of a watermelon wedged inside my belly. My legs became globs of Jell-O, and my insides twisted and groaned. How could I escape? I reflected on an October memory, an excursion with a friend to the hotel when it was the Halloween funhouse. The only exit allowed was by way of a wide slide on this upper floor. Was it still here? Tingles of fear caused my adrenaline to spike. I spun around, then backed up to squeeze my body behind the African grays, hoping my destination was still there. As I crowded closer to Percy, my leg muscles tightened. Then I saw it – a sparkling silver plank just a few feet ahead. What a beautiful sight it was, silently waiting for me. *Be brave, Cassandra. He won't shoot you here.*

"You can't escape," snarled the sinister minister. "Will those birds protect you? No. You're trapped. Come out, or I'll shoot you and the macaw."

Could I move fast enough before the guy shot? What if I slipped and fell? What if he killed Percy? What if the slide had been dismantled part-way down?

My alternative was to raise my hands and take whatever punishment awaited. "Don't shoot," I said. "I'm coming out."

Instead of doing that, I scurried ahead, propelling my legs onto the silver metal, struggling to force my body to travel fast. Down, down, down, I sped, leaning into the curves of the device. Then I bent forward to slow down but plummeted into the air, crashing hard when I landed. As the third floor zoomed past, my speed increased. When I held onto the sides, I slowed down, but gunshots from above pinged against the metal. I trembled, fearing a bullet might hit me. Leaning forward again, I whizzed past the second floor. The first floor was ahead, cluttered with tall stacks of furniture that had replaced the Halloween landing mattresses. Tucking my chin into my neck, I pressed both feet against the slide and closed my eyes.

Wham! Bang! My feet rammed into furniture that tumbled around me like dominoes. An edge of a chest scraped my arms before I landed on a stack of dusty, ragged mats. My legs stuck under a recliner until I tugged them loose. Both of my legs and arms had scratches, and one shoe was gone. But the only serious injury was my ripped and blood-stained slacks.

"Ouch! Never doing that again," I said out loud.

Gunshots and cursing drifted from an upper floor. When the commotion stopped, Officer Bob shouted, "We're on our way down, but we're taking the stairs!"

Brad appeared and pulled me up. "Are you training to be a circus performer?"

"No, working on being brave."

"You accomplished that. Are you injured?"

"Every inch of my body hurts, but I don't think I broke anything."

Officer Hope joined us with the minister handcuffed between him and Officer Jones. The sinister minister's beady eyes glared at me with contempt. He tried to speak but didn't succeed when one of the officers jerked his arm.

"We're off to the station," said Bob Hope. "Cookie, if you can identify Mrs. Delbert's birds, we'll let Brad transport them back to St. Louis."

"I'll call Geneva," said Brad. "She'll be eager for me to take them home."

Officer Hope explained, "Normally, we don't allow civilians to move stolen property. I've contacted the Humane Society. They will be busy. At least fifty other birds, a few strange-looking turtles, and some exotic snakes are scattered in boxes and cages across the fourth floor."

We all laughed when Percy's squawks intensified. "Cookie's cool. Percy's cool."

"That parrot must really like you," said Brad.

All of us worked to load the birds into a large rental van. I walked over to Brad to say goodbye, lightly touching his arm. Unplanned words popped out of my mouth. "Several Branson shows have area appreciation rates. I can request tickets for us."

"Great idea! I'll text you the best dates for me. Order several. Doesn't matter which ones. I'll pay for them."

His last comment irritated me until I heard Mom in my head. *Don't sweat the small stuff.* I smiled. That was one of her favorite phrases.

That time, I didn't avoid a hug. I leaned into Brad's arms and reached up to twirl his gorgeous hair. It was soft in places but firmer where the white had intruded. All my earlier panic dissipated. When we let go, he lifted my chin and gazed at me.

"Neighbors a block from me are vacationing in June. May I give them your name? They have a security system. St. Louis is a fun city, and we can take in several square dances."

"Do your neighbors have snakes, iguanas, or turtles? I prefer cats and dogs, although birds are okay."

"Just one well-trained, five-year-old Golden named Ringo. You do approve of Goldens, don't you?"

"They're incredible dogs. I'll think about it. What's the worst possible thing that can happen?"

"Nothing bad. Consider it a paid vacation. Call you soon to get my BMW back."

I watched the van drive away before starting the car's ignition. When my cell rang, I pulled into an empty lot to answer it.

"This is Nora's daughter. Polly said to call you."

"How's your mother?" I asked.

"Has a concussion and some scratches. She'll be at my house for a while."

Although her injuries weren't my fault, I didn't want her to be hurt. "May I stop by to see her?"

"Wait a few days. She's furious with you, but ten years from now she'll still be telling stories about how she escaped death."

I giggled, excited to hear Nora's version of her trip down the trash chute at the next lunch bunch gathering.

While stopped, I rang Polly. "Has Albert had his surgery yet?"

"Yep. He's doing great. The doc said there were no complications. He's expected to have a fast recovery."

After that, I hummed the birthday song as I drove six blocks to the police station. Inside, Officer Hope sat at his desk, drinking coffee.

"We've booked Charles Wilson the third," he said.

"Do you know why he chose the Delbert's house to rob?"

"Well, it's confidential, but you need to know. Wilson confessed all his bad deeds in exchange for interesting information. John Delbert planned the theft and agreed to split the profit with Wilson. Dishonest John also filed a claim with the insurance company, but he didn't intend his wife's birds to be stolen. During the last two years, he had purchased three illegally imported parrots to keep his wife happy. Wilson also gave us information on a toucan shipment on its way from Mexico."

"How'd Wilson find me?" I asked.

"Don't know. Maybe from your car tag. The red trucks belonged to him."

"Is Wilson a real minister?"

"Sort of – probably not ordained, but he did pastor a church once. When Delbert and Wilson were involved in a realty scam, he was forced to quit the ministry. Sit down. We need your statement." He handed me a legal pad and pen.

"What about the St. Louis police? Will I be arrested for false information?"

"Nah, they forgave you, but you'll have to testify at both trials, and don't erase those voice mails!"

A prickly, tingling, worried feeling engulfed my body. "What if he makes bail?"

Officer Bob rummaged through the desk for a business card, which he gave to me. "Call me if that no-life bothers you. Gotta keep Jones and me busy."

His reply didn't reassure me, but with two policemen and Brad available, Sparky and I would be okay. On the pad, I wrote all my memories of the duct-tape day and the frightening calls that followed.

Officer Bob said, "Jones and I expect recognition for these arrests. How about you? Will you keep pet sitting?"

"Not sure yet. I'm considering another job in St. Louis. Why?"

"You're my first choice for a pet sitter. Before my wife and I schedule our vacation, I'll check to find out when you're available. We plan to book a cruise to Alaska."

The scary, sinister man was in jail along with his two partners. Officer Bob was now my friend. I thought about how quickly life can change, which reminded me of an important question.

"What kind of pets do you have?"

"One dog, Sargent, a four-year-old Pug. He's a super boy."

Not sure about a noisy Pug, but I was now fond of the quirky policeman. I told Officer Bob goodbye and got up to leave. He picked up his mug to wash down the last bite of a chocolate donut. As I opened the door, I heard him say to himself. "St. Louis, interesting. That gal is a real cool cookie."

I smiled. What was the worst possible thing that could happen if I pet sit a Pug?

~THE END~

If you liked *Cookie, The Pet Sitter: Gobs of Pets Caper,* I would love for you to give me a short review on Amazon! Write what you liked, what amused you, and what made you laugh out loud!

~*Coming Soon!*~

You'll be happy to know more Cookie adventures are in the works! You'll laugh as Cookie finds herself in more predicaments. Her pet sitting escapades are only beginning!

ABOUT THE AUTHOR

Nancy Lewis Shelton's published works include children's and adult short stories, devotions, inspirational pieces, and magazine articles. She has been published in *Chicken Soup for the Soul: Inspiration for Teachers,* the *Guardian Angel* e-zine, *Soltice* anthology, *Creative Collections* anthology, *Upper Room, Fifty-Plus* magazine, and *Ozarks Maturity* magazine. Shelton was one of ten winners in a Guideposts contest, where she won a free trip to New York for a week-long workshop. She is a member of the Springfield Writers' Guild.

Nancy was a public school educator for over thirty years. She has also done part-time pet sitting much of her life. She enjoys volunteering in her church crisis food pantry, senior choir and assists with children's programs. She currently volunteers for the RSVP reading tutor program and coordinates a volunteer storytelling group, "Storytellers of the Ozarks." When she's not writing or volunteering, you will find her digging in the garden, playing bridge, family visits, or reading.

She lives in southwest Missouri with her cat, Fred, and dog, Robin. Her married daughter and six grandchildren are frequent visitors.

Contact: storytellersoftheozarks@gmail.com
Website: www.nancylewisshelton.wordpress.com

Made in the USA
Monee, IL
07 December 2021